INCREASINGLY COMPLICATED

3

CULEBRA CHRONICLES

HALF-PAST 2 PUBLICATIONS

Cover Design: Caroline Marques
Illustrations: Canva.com
Editing: Enchanted Ink Publishing
Book Design and Typesetting: Enchanted Ink Publishing

ISBN: 978-1-963402-09-4 (E-book)
ISBN: 978-1-963402-06-3 (Paperback)

Library of Congress Control Number: 2024914374

WWW.CHRISSYCHICORY.COM

This is dedicated to my darling husband, whose unwavering support and love provide me with the perfect environment to pursue my passion, writing.

INCREASINGLY COMPLICATED

3

CULEBRA CHRONICLES

CHRISSY CHICORY

CHAPTER I
ZADIE

adie let out a soft sigh, her tired eyes drifting up to catch a glimpse of the moon peeking through the cloudy night sky. The colors above were as warm as a cozy blanket, with deep purples and indigos blending together. She leaned against the railing of Mama's porch, taking in the sounds of an owl hooting and frogs croaking in the nearby woods. A charming garden gnome, adorned with a crumpled red hat and delicate bells, sat nestled among fragrant lavender bushes in the tea garden by the porch. Its chimes gently jingled as it coyly peeked through the leaves. Zadie's eyes slowly scanned the faces of her sisters, each with a look of concern and foreboding. Her temples began to throb, as a headache crept its way across her scalp. She released her ponytail, hoping to alleviate the tension, her hair now falling freely around her face.

The night felt endless, but not in the good way, like when you are young and free with no worries. No, tonight, each passing second dragged like a heavy weight in the muggy summer atmosphere. Mama's garden offered her little comfort. It wasn't that it didn't have its charm. But it was a stark contrast to the familiar sounds and smells of her marina. She wished she were in bed already, the rocking of the boat lulling her to sleep. Unfortunately, she could feel the evening was far from over. Too many loose ends left untied. Zadie wasn't one to leave sloppy lines. The disturbing events of the past few hours played an unrelentless loop in her mind. Although a feeling of unease had planted its seed in her chest, growing every second, she would see this night to its proper end.

The original plan for this late night was for she and Babs to comfort their sister, Crickt, after her boyfriend had unceremoniously broken up with her at her friend Caroline's wedding reception. All had been going well. Each of the sisters snuggled into pajamas borrowed from Babs, indulging in creamy scoops of ice cream while Cricket poured out her heart. The warm glow of candlelight had been dancing around them, casting a casual atmosphere until the unexpected interruption of a surprise guest.

Nadine.

Their younger sister, whom everyone thought died at birth, had appeared from the darkness of the forest, and engaged in a heated argument with her twin sister, Babs. All right, not everyone had thought Nadine dead. Babs insisted she could see her, hear her. But none of them had believed her. Joke was on them, right?

Zadie immediately took a dislike to Nadine. She was cold and brash. The display of one-upmanship between Nadine and Babs had freaked her out. She was fine with letting her sisters argue amongst themselves when it was just them, but she would not tolerate that behavior at Mama's house while she was there. Yet, honestly, there wasn't much she could have done. They were way past her in magic abilities.

2

Not only was Zadie reeling from the revelation that her long-lost sister was actually alive, but she also couldn't wrap her head around the fact that Babs had become the summer princess. Who would have ever thought that was possible?

Babs had successfully completed the challenges to join the summer court, but something unexpected had happened afterward. She was crowned the summer princess, chosen by Summer herself, and named the Balancer. And sometime in the process of joining summer, she grew sharp fangs like their Aunt Habina. This revelation would take more than just a few hours to fully comprehend and come to terms with.

To be honest, she hadn't put much thought into the courts or how they worked. She had no reason to believe they had any bearing on their lives, but now — Nadine was from winter, and Babs was a part of summer.

Zadie softly rested her hand on Babs's shoulder. Gwylm, Babs's large wolf companion, sized up Zadie before huffing in acknowledgment. "Please, Babs," Zadie began with a heavy sigh. "Before we go inside to see Mama, use your glamour to disguise your new appearance. Mama will already be surprised enough when she sees Nadine. She can learn about your crown and" — Zadie faltered — "new appearance another time."

Zadie heard a sarcastic laugh from behind her. "Aren't we a bossy one tonight." Nadine tapped her foot on the bottom porch step. Her hand rested lightly on her tight stomach as she rolled her eyes at Zadie. "The mermaid has found her voice. Do you think you actually have something valuable to contribute? Mama isn't your concern, little fish. Isn't it about time you swam away and stayed in Atlantis? Isn't Aunt Maj waiting for you? Go fulfill your own destiny. This situation has nothing to do with you. You are not needed."

"Babs, your twin is insufferable!" Cricket's voice came out all in a rush. Her eyes were still puffy from crying.

Babs bared her teeth. "Nadine being here is not my fault. I didn't ask her to join us. She was sent by the winter court."

"Way to make a girl feel welcome," Nadine mumbled.

Cricket ignored her. "Zadie isn't going anywhere any time soon. And she is needed." Cricket took the steps two at a time and wrapped an arm around Zadie while whispering, "You're always needed."

Zadie fought a grin. "I know. I'm your favorite sister," she whispered. "Admit it."

Cricket giggled, keeping her voice low. "Don't tell Babs."

Babs quipped, "Don't tell Babs what?"

Zadie and Cricket replied in unison, "Nothing!"

Zadie turned to face Nadine. "Take it slow with Mama. You got that, Nadine?"

The four of them stood on the porch. Zadie shuffled her slippers against the wooden planks beneath her feet, hesitant to enter.

Cricket cradled the empty ice cream tubs, accidentally smearing chocolate on her silk nightgown. "Unfortunately, we don't have time to take it slow. Mama owes us answers." She pulled the screen door open with more force than it needed. "Gran and Mama left us in the dark. That choice put us at such a disadvantage. This crazy situation was completely avoidable if they had just trusted us enough to tell us what really happened."

Babs picked up the rant. "That the courts were practically in our backyard." She crossed her arms across her Hello Kitty sweatshirt.

Nadine continued, "And Winter was using Dad as a bargaining chip."

Zadie let out a sigh, her irritation rising. She despised confrontations. She made her way into Mama's kitchen, where the scent of bergamot peach tea filled the air. The serene atmosphere was a welcome change from all the drama with her sisters in the backyard. Heading to the sink, she placed the spoons inside and turned on the tap to rinse them, while Cricket disposed of the empty ice cream containers. Babs deftly turned the stove's burner off beneath the whistling tea kettle and reached toward the cabinet that held the mugs, then stopped mid-reach.

Mama, with her hair hastily pulled back in a messy ponytail and dressed in her satin robe and slippers, bustled into the room. She jumped in surprise at the sight of all the girls standing in her kitchen and laughed. "In from the night so soon?" she mused. "I would have expected ice cream time to take twice as long. I thought to have my evening tea in quiet. How lovely that we will take it together."

Babs looked around the room, her hand falling to rest lightly on Gwylm's large head. Power still rippled from her like aftershock waves from the scuffle with Nadine. Cricket fluttered about, like a wisp of anxiety barely tethered to the ground. Zadie understood her unease. Her stomach was still queasy from what they just witnessed. But they were not what drew their mother's attention. It was Nadine.

Mama took a step back and stumbled, her mouth dropped open wide. She began to fold in on herself. Nadine rushed, clutching Mama's limp form, keeping her from hitting the ground. "It can't be." Mama's voice trembled as she looked from Babs's frozen form to Nadine, who held her tenderly.

Zadie's heart ached. She had been wrong all these years—they all had been wrong. Babs claimed that their sister, Nadine, was still alive and often spoke to her. But the entire family had dismissed it, causing endless fights with Babs. Now, as Zadie looked on at Nadine, in flesh and blood, no longer an apparition only seen by Babs, she judged herself for dismissing her sister's claims. It all would have been easier to handle if Nadine hadn't turned out to be so — mean.

Mama's eyes widened. "I need to sit down," she murmured.

Zadie nodded to Cricket to grab the tea kettle. She helped Nadine usher their mom to a chair at the kitchen table. Babs passed out mugs, and Cricket carefully filled them all before gliding into her own chair.

Mama took a moment to gather herself. She placed a quivering hand over Nadine's. "Is it really you?" She stuttered, reaching up to caress Nadine's tear-streaked cheek. "I didn't know you were alive. I didn't know!" she sobbed.

"Mama," Nadine began, "it's not your fault. The winter court . . . they took me. Dad's there too." Her silver eyes held such joy. "I'm going to bring him back to you, Mama. I just need to find the winter princess's crown."

Mama wailed, startling everyone at the table. "I know he's alive. The druids allowed me to gaze in the pool at Avalon. I could see his form, feel him." Sobs shook her entirely. "That's why I was away so often." She wiped at her tears. "There's no hope of ever bringing him home, but at least I could see him through the pool, with aid."

Cricket stood up, her chair flying to the ground behind her. "You knew he was alive and didn't tell us?" It was more of an accusation than a question. "How could you?" She slammed her fists down on the table, causing her tea to spill.

Mama's face turned white. "He is lost to this world," she whispered, her eyes darting back to Nadine. "But you! How were you vailed from me?"

All eyes landed on Nadine. What inside knowledge did she have from the winter court?

"The summer lady stole me from my crib and cast a forgetting spell on all. She delivered me to the winter court. What deal she had with the king is beyond my knowledge. I am under the orders of Prince Ambrosias to stay by Babs's side. My time at court has made me strong. I will find the crown and return it to the court, and in return Father will be released, and we will live here together, a happy family."

Mama glanced around the room, her voice falling to a whisper. "The crown was hidden beyond our reach."

Zadie's brows knotted in confusion. She leaned in closer, laying a gentle hand on Mama's shoulder. Mama's gaze flitted to the windows, to the shadows clinging to the corners. "Mama, what is it?"

"Spies," Mama breathed out, almost inaudible. "Both courts have them, lurking, listening. We must be cautious, for the walls themselves may gather our whispers." Her eyes darted about, seeking invisible threats amongst the familiar trappings of home.

The weight of Mama's paranoia settled upon them, a tangible presence that sucked the warmth from the kitchen. It coiled around Zadie's thoughts. Was Mama right? Was this a clandestine war waged in the shadows. Or was her mother paranoid?

Zadie nudged a half-empty teacup toward the center of the large wooden table, her movements deliberate as she sought to dispel the chill that her mother's words had cast over the room.

Cricket's chair groaned as she righted it and sat back down. "Mama, you have to tell us everything. Dad is alive, and you've known where he was all along." Her voice rose in volume, and there was a sharp edge to it that made

Zadie's neck hairs stand on end. "Don't we deserve to know what is going on?"

Mama's voice was quiet and cautious, as if even the air around them could betray their secret. She explained, "Our family played a part in hiding the crown. Maj had it last. At Gran's behest, it was taken to Atlantis."

"Atlantis?" Zadie echoed, a note of alarm threading through her voice. Her shoulders drooped with the weight of understanding that settled upon her like an anchor to the deep. The city beneath the waves—the realm of her destiny—whispered its calling into the fabric of her being.

"I'm not ready . . ." Zadie faltered, her thoughts adrift in the ocean of what lay ahead. A foreboding sense crept into her heart, a certainty that the path before her would lead away from the shores of her current life. Once her feet touched the submerged streets of Atlantis, the part of her that walked among the mortal world would be lost, like sea foam dissolving into the endless blue.

"Girls, it was done to save you," Mama said, reaching across the table to clasp Zadie's hand.

The flickering candlelight cast a dance of shadows across Mama's face, revealing the lines of worry that had etched themselves deeper into her features. She took a slow breath, steadying herself before she spoke again, her voice carrying the weight of painful memories. "There is a prophecy, the telling," Mama began, her eyes darting to each daughter in turn, "that has haunted our line for generations. 'Sister against sister shall mark the rise and fall of the ruling crowns.' Gran never wanted us entangled in such darkness. I don't know how it all began, but Gran decided this was the only way."

The words *sister against sister* echoed ominously through the room.

"That's not the exact wording." Nadine's brow furrowed in skepticism. "Why did Gran believe the telling was about the Culebra line? All the great family lines have sisters. The telling could just as well be about the Daughters of Inanna instead of us."

Babs stood up, her purple hair falling like a royal curtain kissing her shoulders. "Our family or not," she declared, her tone unyielding, "we have a reason to get involved. Get Dad back by getting the crown. Simple."

With a nod, Zadie gave in to the path that was laid before her. Her destiny, intertwined with Atlantis and the crown concealed within its depths, was calling her home. "The tides of fate pull us out to sea. What's the point of fighting them?" She shrugged, a frown settling on her face. "In the morning, we meet at the marina. I will have *Yara* ready for the voyage."

"Good." Babs nodded. "We move quickly. Make sure to wrap up any loose ends before morning."

The room fell into a charged silence, each sister lost in her own thoughts.

"I'm sorry," Mama said, breaking the hush with a note of desperation. "We tried to keep all of this from touching you. We tried to shield you from it. Leaving the courts should have worked. Raising you in the mortal world, it should have spared you."

Zadie's eyes wandered to the window, where the luminous moonlight shone through. She sensed that this night was crucial, a turning point between what had come before and what would come after. She wondered if her family would make it through this experience unscathed.

"I'm heading back to Baubles and Whatnots," Cricket declared. "Hopefully Gran will fill me in on everything she knows about the crown."

Mama carefully wrapped a plate of cookies in a worn tea towel. "Take these to her," she instructed, her voice thick with emotion. "Tell her . . . tell her I'll call in the morning. There is much to discuss." She stole a glance at Nadine.

Cricket accepted the offering, her delicate fingers brushing against Mama's. As Cricket turned to leave, Zadie caught a shimmer in her sister's eyes—a mix of exhaustion and anxiety.

The screen door closed, and Zadie was left with Nadine still sitting at the table. As their eyes met, a thousand questions hung in the air between them. Zadie's gaze held a mix of emotions: happiness at finding out her long-lost sibling was alive, and trepidation. The conflicting feelings of curiosity and distrust churned within Zadie as she tried to make sense of this stranger who was also her own flesh and blood.

Nadine's lips curved upward ever so slightly, a wisp of a smile that reminded Zadie of a wolf. Zadie vowed to herself that she would face this new world, where allies were indistinguishable from foes, with eyes wide open.

"Let's not keep destiny waiting," Nadine murmured, drawing Zadie out of the silence.

Zadie fought back tears.

Babs started up the stairs. "Nadine, follow me. I'll show you around my old room. I'm sure it will have everything you need." Their footfalls echoed off the wooden steps. "I think Cricket left Aunt Habina's spell book in my room. You might like looking it over." Babs's voice trailed off.

Zadie moved about the kitchen with silent grace, her hands deftly clearing the remnants of their hurried evening tea from the table. The scent of bergamot still lingered in the air, a comforting aroma. She swept cookie crumbs into her palm, her movements meticulous but tender, as if each piece she picked up held a fragment of the past she was desperate to preserve. Mama stood by the window, her gaze lost in the sprawl of their garden.

"Be careful." Mama's voice was barely audible, a whisper woven with worry. "The courts are treacherous, more than you could possibly imagine."

Zadie paused, her hands hovering above the sink now full of sudsy water. "The courts are of no concern to me, as you know." What was so horrible that Mama had doomed herself to years of loss and yearning? "I wish you would have told us about Father. Told us about the crown."

Mama turned, her eyes meeting Zadie's. "It wasn't your burden to bear. It was our problem to solve. Mine. Gran's. Maj's."

Zadie folded the dishcloth with precise corners and laid it to rest beside the sink. The room settled into a hushed stillness. The ticking of the clock on the wall marked the moments slipping away. "I'm sure you did what you thought best. But we are going to finish this — our way." There was no room for doubt, not when so much rested on their shoulders — the hope of her family, the yearning of her Mama's heart.

With a practiced touch, she withdrew her phone from her purse, the screen lighting up her features in a soft glow. Her thumbs danced over the keyboard with an urgency that betrayed her calm exterior. She crafted a message to her boyfriend Tom.

> Zadie: Can you meet me tonight? Need to see you.

The text sent, she slipped the phone away, and silence reclaimed the space around her. The digital words, now adrift in the ether, carried a weight far heavier than their simple characters could convey. The reality of parting from Tom made her feel heavy. Sick. Yet even as her heart ached for the life she knew she must leave behind, the call of her Mer lineage surged within her.

Her feet led her to the door, and her hand found solace in the cool metal of the doorknob. With a confident twist and a soft push, she stepped out into the night that awaited her. Standing on the threshold, she felt suspended between two worlds: the comfort of home behind her and the vast unknown stretching before her.

Zadie squared her shoulders, feeling the power of her heritage rise to meet the challenge. She was Culebra, fae of sea. Nothing could save her from the course set by destiny. She whispered over her shoulder, "Goodbye, Mama."

CHAPTER 2
BABS

The swamp was a chorus of whispers and croaks, as Babs focused on the task at hand. She stepped forward, her shoes sinking slightly into the soft earth, a terrain she had grown accustomed to in response to Liande's numerous summonings. Moonlight danced a pale glow over the thick vegetation that clung to the edge of this reality.

Phasing in and out of different locations had become routine for her. She reminisced about how challenging it had been when she first started learning this skill. Now, she no longer needed vibrational bars to guide her to the correct frequency, nor did she feel sick from not matching the frequency perfectly. It had become effortless; all she had to do was think of where she wanted to go, and the world around her shifted accordingly.

Her ability to cast spells had grown exponentially, and she no longer needed to utter a word. Instead, just by visualizing her intention in her mind's eye, she could make it come to life.

The tranquility of being away from Nadine's challenging presence was a welcomed reprieve. She finally accepted that Nadine was truly her sister and actually alive. Gone was Nadine's translucent form and eerie aura that had haunted Babs for so long. Nadine was now a flesh-and-blood being, who had been used as a pawn in a twisted political game orchestrated by the winter court.

Despite being twins, they clashed like two opposing forces — oil and water. Nadine had a knack for tormenting her, always finding ways to disrupt her peace. But despite their differences, they were now bound together by a common objective: to bring their father back from the grasp of winter's cold embrace. The well-being of their family was the one thing that could bridge the gap between them and unite them in purpose.

Gwylm was diligently keeping an eye on Nadine at Mama's house. Babs felt a sense of relief knowing his towering form shadowed Nadine's every move as she got accustomed to her new surroundings. His sharp amber eyes, ever watchful for any signs of things amiss, gave Babs comfort. His massive wolflike frame radiated strength and security, surely making Mama feel safe and reassured.

As Babs approached the murky pond, the glowing amber of alligator eyes pierced through the darkness. They were Liande's silent protectors, stationed at the entrance to her mystical realm. The stillness of the water and the rustling of nearby trees created an eerie atmosphere, as if time ran differently in this enchanted place. Babs felt a sense of foreboding and curiosity as she stood before these creatures, wondering what secrets they held within their unblinking gazes.

Babs called out. Her voice steady, cloaking her fatigue,

"Liande!" Her eyes widened as a chilling vision manifested before her.

With skin that mimicked the armored hide of her reptilian kin, Liande's figure was both seductive and terrifying. Gentle ripples rode the surface of the pond as her tail swayed steadily in the water.

Ethereal figures swirled about Liande. Their translucent forms twisted in tumultuous screams. The stolen spirits of St. Augustine encircled the fae, their agony a haunting melody that amplified Liande's already formidable powers. Babs could feel the magic pulsing in the air, a tangible force that thrummed with every ghostly wail.

Babs's confusion gave way to a dawning realization. It was Liande who had orchestrated the theft of souls. She had played Bash like a pawn. The portal that had drained St. Augustine of its lingering dead had been her doing.

"Cricket will never forgive this!" Babs spat in outrage. Her sister's love for Bash had been palpable, and the thought of Cricket discovering this treachery turned her stomach.

"When your sister is crowned winter princess, our dominion will no longer be her concern." Liande's clawed fingers scratched idly at the water's edge. "However, I will send them back to where they came from — once they have fulfilled their purpose." She licked at her lips, then added, "For you."

Babs gave a small nod of appreciation. Though she and Liande were not exactly close, Liande's expression of respect meant everything to her.

The weight of the summer crown pressed heavily upon Babs's brow. Its ancient power pulsed through her, the voices of long-gone rulers whispering urgently in the recesses of her mind. *Heed us*, they hissed, their words like serpents slithering through the undergrowth of her consciousness. *Use us. Release our power.* Babs took a deep breath, filling her lungs to their capacity, and then slowly released it, hoping to calm the racing voices in her head.

Liande's voice was velvet over steel. "Yes, I see what goes on behind your eyes. The crown suits you." She reached forward, her clawed fingers brushing against Babs's arm with surprising gentleness. The contact sparked a glow from the intricate symbols that adorned their skin, a visible testament to the pact they had forged. A web of light danced between them, binding their fates together with threads of ancient magic. "Remember, without my intervention, you would not stand here as the summer princess. It was I who set you upon this path—a path that leads to greatness for both of us. You have changed much," Liande murmured, and Babs could not miss the approval in her tone. "When the moment arrives, reach for me. With these spirits' aid, I shall draw you to my side, and together, we will reshape this weakened realm."

Babs watched as the shimmering glyphs on her arm mirrored those on Liande's. This connection was more than a simple alliance; it was a promise of ascension, a future where she might stand shoulder to shoulder with Liande, unfettered by the constraints of the current queen.

Babs straightened, the crown's influence molding her resolve into something hard and bright as a diamond. "Then let that moment come swiftly."

Liande paced the perimeter of the pool. The alligators watched with lazy menace. "Should we fail to deliver the crown to the winter king"—her voice was a silky hiss that carried through the humid air—"you stand to lose more than your position."

"If we succeed?" Babs asked.

A fierce grin spread across Liande's face, revealing a row of jagged teeth. "Power, dominion over all the summer lands . . . and I swear by the old blood of Inanna, you shall be my equal in all things."

The symbols on their arms flickered like embers at the mention of the ancient goddess, reinforcing the potency of Liande's oath.

Taking a slow breath, Babs replied, "I give you my oath, Liande, Daughter of Inanna. I shall help you achieve this end."

Liande intoned, "Your word, sealed by the ancients." As their symbols met, the light flared brilliant and pure.

"With the power of those before me" — she reached up and touched the edge of her crown — "together, we shall bring forth a new era, or fall to ruin trying."

"Let the spirits of the dead witness our covenant," Liande declared, her arm linked with Babs's as the eerily whispering ghosts swirled around them, their moans a howling chorus.

Babs's fingers traced the still-warm sigils etched into her arm, their glow fading like the last embers of a dying fire. The air was thick with the low hum of nocturnal life that thrived within the swamp's embrace.

"Liande." Babs's voice betrayed a tremor she wished to hide. "The crown whispers — "

"Such is the nature of fae crowns," Liande replied, her voice low. "They seduce with promises of what could be. Look how cold the crown turned my sister, Sabella." Liande's gaze settled on the murky waters. "But remember, we are not mere vessels for their desires. We shape our fate."

"Yet what of my sister, Cricket? If she is destined to be the princess of winter—" Babs asked, wrestling with concern. She would not be a part of anything that would damn her sister.

"You worry of your sister's fate? Look into the pool, Babs." With a languid motion, Liande stirred the waters, coaxing forth images from its depths. "See the vision that has graced me. It will grant you clarity."

Babs watched, her breath caught in her throat as impressions emerged from the ripples. There, amidst the spectral light, was Ambrosias, resplendent and regal, placing the winter crown upon Cricket's head. A smile of genuine happiness lit Cricket's face, a drastic contrast to the haunting visions that had tormented Babs's imagination.

A pang of relief softened Babs's stance. "Cricket seems content."

Liande continued to manipulate the waters. The scene shifted, revealing a new destiny—the throne room where Babs stood by Liande's side, the full might of her position as summer princess radiating from her very being. Power pulsed around them, tangible and intoxicating. Queen Sabella would never respect her in that way. If she remained regent, Babs would be little more than a servant. And there, amidst the courtly splendor, was a figure Babs had never seen—a fae prince of such beauty that it struck a chord deep within her, awakening a fierce curiosity.

Babs found herself asking, unable to tear her eyes away from the apparition, "Who is he?"

"A future ally, perhaps more . . . if we succeed," Liande intoned, her eyes gleaming with the reflection of the water's magic. "A prince who seeks a princess of equal strength. I feel the hunt on the move. Soon the summer king will return with all his men, and the court will be whole again."

Babs had never met the men of the court. The king had been gone when she started her training. How different would things be with a king by Liande's side?

"What are they like? The summer king and his men?"

Liande's smile was a rare vision, lighting up her eyes like crystals in a cave. "The summer king is like life itself," she said, her voice filled with admiration and reverence. "The earth responds to his very touch, blooming and thriving under his every footstep." Her eyes sparkled with excitement as she spoke of seeing him once again. "He is noble and kind."

Babs picked at her cuticle. "And the summer prince?"

Liande's expression softened slightly at the mention of the prince, a hint of something akin to regret flickering in her glowing eyes. "The prince will have his own role to play in all of this. I see him in your future. You will share a special bond," she replied cryptically, swaying in the water. "But first, we must secure the crown."

"Is this truly possible? Can this be our future?" Babs's heart raced.

"Only if we deliver the crown to the winter king," Liande said, her voice resonating with certainty. "Our destinies intertwine, Babs. Together, we can ascend to heights untold."

The summer crown upon Babs's head hummed with an ancient energy, its magic weaving through her being, altering her essence in fundamental ways. She could feel the power of the rulers who had come before her, seeping into her skin, altering not just her mind but her very destiny.

"Power is not given lightly," murmured a voice from within the crown, resonant and multi-layered, as if a chorus of predecessors spoke as one. "We offer it to you willingly."

"Then I shall be your vessel," she whispered, her voice steady despite the cacophony of counsels in her head. Even as the crown urged her toward a path of ascension, Babs knew that the true test lay in balancing her new position within the summer court and her duties as a sister, a daughter, a woman of the Culebra line. That realization anchored her, even as possibilities danced tantalizingly in her vision.

She glanced back at the pool, watching as the water began to stir once more, images swirling with the promise of futures untold. For the first time, she saw them clearly without Liande's guiding hand — the countless threads of what might be, each glowing with the potential of the summer crown's power. Her power. It was a revelation that shook her to her core, a glimpse into the vast expanse of capabilities. Her capabilities.

The voices coaxed, *Imagine the worlds you could shape, the realms you could bind to your will*, their whispers growing fervent, almost desperate. *You were born for this. For greatness*, they continued.

With each shallow breath, she could feel the push and pull of mounting desires — visions flashing before her eyes with such rapidity it was dizzying. Dreams of grandeur each more vast than the next. The crown on her head felt both like a mantle of destiny and a privilege. Her privilege.

Power. The voices were no longer hushed but clamoring for attention. *Rule. Conquer. Ascend.* Their cacophony was a tempest whirling her deeper into the realm of ambition.

Babs pressed her palms against her temples, trying to silence the voices that constantly tormented her. She longed for a day when she wouldn't have to struggle so hard to keep them in check.

With a flick of her mind, she shifted her focus from within to without, sensing a delicate enchantment cradling her in a soothing haze.

The full moon's ethereal light bathed the rippling and dancing surface of the water. Liande's voice, low and soothing, bewitched Babs. "This is what our future holds," Liande said. In the pool, a vision of Babs's and Liande's future selves appeared—not just a reflection but a glimpse into what was to come. Babs exuded an air of regal composure and natural authority, her slender figure radiating a magnetic charm.

As she stared at herself in the reflection in the water, she could feel the allure of control pulling at her very being. The idea of being a mighty ruler, on par with Liande and revered by the entire court, filled her with an intense longing. Her nipples grew taut at the intoxicating possibility. Butterflies danced happily in her stomach, as she eagerly envisioned the triumph and glory that awaited her in this moment.

A soft moan escaped from her parted lips, as if surrendering to the delicious sensations coursing through her. With deliberate slowness, she ran her hand over her curves, reveling in the sensation of her own touch on the most sensitive places of her body.

In the stillness of the night, Liande's voice was but a whisper. "Yes, power is indeed seductive and sensual. I can feel it emanating from you; it's intoxicating. Entrancing." Her gaze never left Babs's movements as she spoke, mirroring them with her own gestures. As their desires simulated one another in perfect harmony, Babs's own passion grew stronger.

A distant howl pierced the night, a solitary sound that seemed to encapsulate her rapture. The crown pulsed atop her head, its magic threading through her consciousness, weaving visions of power and dominion that sounded all too enticing, all too alluring.

Babs gasped, transfixed, the potential paths fanning out before her like the roots of an ancient tree. The murmur escaped her lips, a prayer to the fates that spun the threads of future and past, "Yes."

CHAPTER 3
ZADIE

Zadie leaned casually against the bow pulpit on the deck of her ship, wrapped in her well-worn cotton robe, feet bare. Her arms rested lightly on the polished wooden railing. She leaned over the edge, addressing *Yara* and *Dulcinea* — the masthead sisters who were bonded to the vessel. They had once been mermaids, living in the vast ocean until they were kidnapped by pirates and forced to serve as figureheads, bound forever, navigating the dangerous waters. Their entwined arms and long, sensual hair floated gracefully over the soft waves that melodically rocked the boat in the marina. "I'm sorry to ask this of you." Zadie sighed. "My sisters will arrive before dawn. We must be ready to set sail at first light."

Yara's even voice penetrated Zadie's mind. "*I didn't expect us to take this voyage for some time yet. Will you be coming back with us?*"

Dulcinea sighed. "*Atlantis.*" Her inflection was full of desire. "*What I wouldn't give to walk those streets again — dip my hands in the pools of memory.*"

Yara mused, "*I should like to lay eyes upon the water dragons one more time.*"

Zadie nodded sympathetically, fully comprehending their longing. "I only have this evening to say goodbye to Tom. It's highly probable that you will be returning without me." Zadie ran her hand along the bottom of the mainsail, checking the seams for any wear. "Can I rely on you to bring my sisters back safely once our task is complete?"

The melancholic splashes of a nearby fish caught Zadie's attention, and she turned her head in search of the sound.

Yara's voice was hesitant. "*Yes,*" she agreed. "*We will do as you ask, Zadie.*"

Zadie prepared herself for the journey ahead, determined not to let her sadness consume her. She blew out a deep breath, letting it tickle her lips, and said, "Thank you."

With focused intention, *Yara* and *Dulcinea* followed Zadie's lead and weaved intricate spells into the very wood of the ship. Magical energy crackled through every inch, strengthening the vessel for its treacherous voyage ahead. As their enchantments took hold, the sails billowed with renewed vigor, and the hull shone with an otherworldly glow. They imbued the ship with powerful protections, making ready for even the harshest elements of the sea.

When the readying of the ship was done, Zadie's eyes lingered longingly on the sparkling lights coming from the lively restaurants across the street as night cloaked all in shadow. She could just make out the distant strains of a jazz band playing in the background. The memories of drifting off to sleep to the comforting melodies of Old Town brought a warm smile to her lips. This marina, this community, had been her home, and she had treasured every moment of it.

"Zadie." *Dulcinea's* tone broke the spell of Zadie's lingering thoughts. "*Have you been to Atlantis?*"

Zadie sighed. "No. I have never been there, only felt its calling."

"Then there's something you need to know about where we're headed." Dulcinea's voice was tentative.

Zadie pulled her gaze away from the busy street. "What is it?"

"The Bermuda Triangle," Dulcinea revealed, her timbre heavy with the weight of her words. *"We will have to cross the Bermuda Triangle to get to Atlantis. We risk getting lost in time."*

Zadie's face scrunched up in a frown, and her stomach plummeted. She couldn't deny the truth of it. The work done beneath the ocean's surface in Atlantis caused disturbances, tears in the fabric of time. Countless vessels — ships and airplanes — had disappeared in the Bermuda Triangle, never to be seen again. She could not doom her sisters or her vessel to such a fate.

Yara's voice was filled with concern as she responded, *"Unfortunately, the Triangle is a sorrowful consequence of the responsibility they carry in Atlantis."*

Dulcinea chimed in, *"As below, so above. The water dragons dictate the direction for us all."*

Zadie reasoned, "Aunt Maj will answer our call," her voice steady. "There's no need to fret."

"Permission to come aboard, Captain!" Tom's familiar voice called out from the dock, causing a smile to cross Zadie's face. "I was happy to see your text, Zadie, although surprised."

Yara and *Dulcinea's* voices went silent, giving Zadie privacy.

Tom's silhouette was half-hidden, carved out by the play of shadows against his muscular frame. "You have *Dulcinea* in ship shape," Tom praised.

Zadie drew slow, languid circles on the polished wood deck with her left foot, channeling her energy into the movement, using it to calm her breath, willing her shoulders to relax. She didn't wish to infect Tom with her melancholy. He joined her, his eyes bright with a sparkle of mischief. She was determined to make this night a beautiful one, a perfect memory that they both could cherish.

Zadie lifted her head to meet his gaze. "I set sail tomorrow."

Tom grinned, a marvelous sight that made her stomach clinch. "What adventure are you off on now, my little dare devil?" He lifted his palm in the air. "Don't tell me. Let me guess." He rubbed the slight stubble at his chin. "Are you finally taking my suggestion and embarking on the Great Loop? You've sailed the ocean, but now you hone your delicate boating skills. Complete the six-thousand-mile journey around the Atlantic, Gulf Intracoastal Waterway, Great Lakes, Canadian Heritage Canals, and inland rivers of America's heartland." He gestured with his hands, tracing an invisible map of the continent that was deeply ingrained in his memory. "It's a complete circle that ends with the reward of reaching the Florida Keys. Just imagine, Zadie, you'll finally be a 'Looper.' And there's no sight quite like seeing the Statue of Liberty as you approach New York. Think about all those who crossed the Atlantic to catch a glimpse of her shining face, full of hope and looking to start a new life."

Zadie reached for his hand and intertwined her fingers with his, pulling it toward her lips for a gentle kiss. Her heart ached at the touch of him, her breath hitching in her chest. A rush of memories cascaded through her mind, each one more intoxicating than the last. She could vividly recall the endless nights they spent tangled in each other's embrace, their bodies moving in perfect sync as Tom's skilled hands slowly explored every inch of her body. "My keel is too deep to do the loop, Tom. I would run aground in so many places." She gestured to the sails that towered above their heads like billowing clouds. "*Yara* towers way above nineteen feet. We would never fit beneath the bridges." Her voice caught in her throat, as if she had swallowed shards of glass. "Wrong boat, Tom, wrong girl."

He tilted his head to one side, sensing her dark mood. "So then, not the Loop — right now." He lifted her chin delicately with one thick finger and traced the line of her throat. "Someday we will do the Loop together, on my boat. We can set the autopilot and drink, laugh, and dream together while we float by the ever-changing landscape."

Desire stirred within her, his enthusiasm sparking a longing in her heart. This part of him, this addiction to living, was what drew her to give herself over to him, indulging in the most delicious adventures and pleasures. She had never felt more fulfilled than by being at his side, in all ways physically and emotionally.

"Tom." She let his name drip from her tongue. Tonight, she would devour him. Like a ravenous beast, she would take him in greedily, again and again. His body would be her feast, his moans her sustenance. She would possess him completely, in a fiery dance of desire. She wanted to burn his image into her mind, to savor the taste and feel of him.

With his strong jaw and sun-kissed skin, he looked like a man who had faced storms and come out stronger on the other side. "Zadie girl, if not the Loop, where are you off to?" He ran his fingers through her hair, his eyes alight with desire. The moon cast a soft glow over their entwined bodies, highlighting every curve and angle. This was her last night on land — her last night with him. She couldn't tell him the whole truth, but how could she explain without revealing too much? "I wish we had more time, but things happened so quickly." She hungrily pressed herself against him, inhaling deeply the familiar scent of salt and sandalwood that always drove her wild. "I'm taking my sisters out for a deep-sea voyage. We will be gone for quite some time." She couldn't bring herself to tell him that she wouldn't be coming back.

Zadie couldn't look away from his captivating form. She traced her fingers through his hair and balled them into fists, tugging on it. "Tom, I—" Zadie hesitated, her heart pounding in her chest.

With teasing nips and fiery kisses, she traced a path along his jawline, feeling his ragged breaths quicken in response. His passion fueled hers. She tried to hold back the tears that threatened to fall, but they only added to how intoxicating he tasted on her tongue, his arousal a palpable reaction to her touch.

"Zadie," Tom breathed, his voice low and husky as he spun her around with a fierce grip on her waist. She could feel the heat of his body pressed against her back, igniting a wild desire within her. His hand slid up under her loose robe, tracing the curve of her spine as his other hand cupped her breast. His teeth grazed her earlobe, sending pleasure rippling through her body. "I see the readiness of your ship," he murmured, his breath hot against her skin. "I feel the readiness of your body." His touch became more intense, his fingers delving deeper as she pressed against his hand. Their bodies moved in unison like the ebb and flow of the ocean. The world around them faded into a blur as her focus narrowed to the sensations elicited by his familiar touch. Her desire flowed freely. She surrendered completely to the pleasure he gave.

"I'll give you a proper send-off," he groaned heavily.

His mouth trailed the line of her jaw as he turned her to face him. Their lips met in a hungry, desperate kiss. "Zadie, my love," he whispered against her lips, his voice filled with devotion. "Return to me. Go, as you must—but return to me."

The salt-tinged sea breeze tousled Tom's hair, lending him the air of a rugged adventurer as his fingers trailed down the soft curve of her waist, teasing and taunting as she pulled away. He tugged at the sash of her robe, exposing her body for his eyes to devour. His lips curled into a smile as his gaze, filled with a predatory hunger, locked onto her like a magnet. The depths of his eyes were dark and all-consuming. Her skin was alight with longing, every nerve on edge in desperate need of his touch. Her body ached to be consumed by him.

She trailed her fingers along his chest, undoing each button with purpose and precision. Her touch was like fire on his skin. With every kiss she placed on his exposed flesh, his body trembled with longing for more.

The fabric of her well-worn robe brushed against her skin like feathers, caressing her body. Her fingers traced the outline of his shorts. With tantalizing slowness, she undid the button and zipper. He couldn't contain his pleasure as she wrapped her hands around him.

A moan escaped her lips as she felt his warm breath on her skin. He lowered his head, his teeth teasing and caressing her breast with skilled movements. She closed her eyes and let out a gasp, surrendering to the intense sensations he was causing with just his mouth.

"Make tonight unforgettable," she pleaded, her voice trembling as he trailed kisses down her body. "I leave for my voyage in the morning."

Zadie whispered into Tom's ear, as their breathing grew ragged and urgent. "I need you." As they lost themselves in each other, Zadie felt a mixture of overwhelming love for Tom and the crushing weight of the impending separation.

Tom gasped, his voice cracking with emotion. "Tonight, you will have your fill." He lifted her into his arms and carried her to the small cabin below the deck of the boat. Their lips fused.

As they stumbled into the cozy cabin, Tom kicked the door shut and gently laid Zadie on the bed. Her hands moved to pull him on top of her, eager to feel his skin against hers, feel his weight on her.

Zadie lost herself in the moment. All that mattered was the man in front of her. They moved in a perfect rhythm as they explored each other's skin with eager hands and hungry mouths.

She shuddered under his expert touch, every nerve ending alight with. His hands were urgent, exploring every curve and dip. She moaned with delight as his lips moved with precision, knowing exactly how to bring her pleasure. In this moment, there was no thought of separation, only the overwhelming connection as he entered her. Zadie let out a low cry of heightened ecstasy.

Tom's muscles tensed and trembled with pleasure in response to Zadie's climax. His moans were deep and guttural, escaping from his lips as his pleasure was unleashed. "Zadie," he whispered hoarsely.

The tears were warm and salty against Zadie's cheeks as they fell from her eyes. Tom's hands cradled her face with tenderness. As his lips pressed against her skin, she could feel the warmth of his breath against her face. Desire sated, his touch had turned gentle and soothing. In this moment, she felt truly seen and loved for who she was.

She rested her head on his chest, listening to the rhythm of his breathing gradually slow down until she knew he had fallen into a peaceful slumber. She raised her head and gazed at him, committing every aspect of his face to memory. The gentle moonlight made him appear innocent and vulnerable.

"I will remember you like this," she whispered.

CHAPTER 4

CRICKET

Cricket lingered by the window of Baubles and Whatnots, her gaze lost in the dance of dust motes caught in a shaft of the moonlight. Her fingers absentmindedly traced the edge of an ancient coin pendant that was finely displayed in the window as she glanced at her phone for what must have been the hundredth time that evening. No new messages. She let out a heavy sigh, feeling deflated by Bash's silence. All she wanted was reassurance that he was okay and that they could still be friends despite their breakup. Yes — she was being needy. She knew she needed to give him space, but it felt like an eternity had already passed since their talk. Her heart was heavy, and she couldn't shake the all-consuming feeling of misery.

The antique store, like a time capsule bursting at the seams, felt suffocatingly cramped. Its towering shelves, laden with an array of treasures from decades past, seemed to be bending under the weight of it all. Every nook and cranny was occupied by some strange or intriguing object — old books with yellowed pages, delicate porcelain figurines, tarnished silver teapots. The air was thick with the scent of aging wood and musty fabrics. It was as if the store itself were holding its breath.

The breakup at Caroline's wedding had been a harsh awakening for her. In hindsight, she realized that her relationship with Bash had been fizzling out for a while now. With the duties of being maid of honor absorbing all her time and energy, it had been easy to push aside the nagging feeling in her heart that things were not okay. But seeing Caroline and Michael together reminded her of what true love looked like, and she couldn't deny that it was something she'd never had with Bash. She regretted that the fervor wasn't there. But deep down she knew they were better off as friends. He had been right to end it. But did she have to lose him entirely?

A thin layer of cold sweat coated her body, causing her to shiver. How could something as simple as nerves have such a powerful grip on her body? Being left with her own thoughts was driving her looney.

Ambrosias, the winter prince, had vanished into an uncomfortable silence just when his counsel would've been welcomed. Passion. She most defiantly felt passion for Ambrosias. But could she trust him? He had known all along about her father's plight within the winter court—yet chose to keep her in the dark. And to make matters worse, Nadine—her own sister—was alive and ensnared in this web of deception. How could he have kept such crucial information from her?

Nadine appeared eager to find a spot in their lives. She and Babs, despite being twins, didn't see eye to eye. Zadie seemed indifferent toward Nadine. Admittedly, Nadine had a rather abrasive personality, most likely due to her existence being denied all these years. Perhaps—just perhaps—Cricket could attempt to make her feel more accepted.

Gran's slippered steps shuffled down the staircase from her apartment above the shop, a steady rhythm that cut through Cricket's melancholy. "I didn't expect you back this evening. I thought you were staying the night with Babs."

Trailing closely behind her was Tikaboo, Cricket's Cavalier King Charles spaniel. Her feathery tail swished back and forth in a joyful rhythm. With eyes gleaming like polished gemstones and a tongue playfully lolling out of her mouth, her face radiated pure delight.

"Sorry to wake you, Gran," Cricket murmured, tucking her phone away and forcing a smile on her face.

"What has put that frown on your face, child?" Gran's voice pulled her back to the moment. Her eyes were heavy with sleep as she peered through her spectacles. Her hand moved gracefully to cover her mouth, suppressing a yawn.

"This is a smile, Gran," Cricket said, pushing her personal drama to the back of her mind. She gently set Mama's plate of cookies down on the counter. The delicate white floral border of her mom's cherished Staffordshire Liberty Blue serving platter was entirely obscured by a teetering mountain of cookies. The aroma of freshly baked goodness wafted through the air.

While Cricket appreciated the allure of the Liberty Blue pattern, she found herself drawn to the gentle elegance of the rose chintz pink design by the Johnson Brothers. Its delicate floral motif and soft hues resonated deeply with her sense of style. Over time, she meticulously assembled a near-complete collection for her own kitchen, each piece adding a touch of refinement to her cozy space. She discovered that even a modest meal of homemade soup, paired with a slice of freshly baked rustic bread, tasted infinitely better when served on fine china. Each dish elevated her dining experience, transforming everyday nourishment into a delightful ritual.

She locked eyes with Gran, her heart heavy with the knowledge that she would have to break the news to her. Cricket's voice wavered as she spoke. "Gran, it's Nadine . . . She's not gone like we thought. She's alive, and she's been held captive by the winter court all these years, along with Dad." The weight of her words hung in the air, accompanied by a heavy silence. A searing wind blew through the room, stirring the curtains and causing them to flutter like wraiths. Gran's expression was veiled. Cricket could see the memories flooding back — the day of Babs's birth and Nadine's supposed death, Dad's disappearance, and the years of mourning that followed.

The lines around Gran's weathered mouth deepening like creases in an ancient map as she took a deliberate step back. Cricket could see Gran's eyes flicker with contemplation, her mind sifting through a lifetime of memories and wisdom, meticulously sorting through every piece of knowledge before deciding what to reveal. "This burden is not yours to carry," she finally said, her voice tinged with fear.

Cricket's eyes widened, reflecting the gravity in her voice. "The winter king has tasked us with finding and returning the lost winter crown," she declared, her voice growing stronger and more resolute with each word. "It's our only hope to free Nadine and Dad from winter's icy clutches. My sisters and I will embark on our quest at dawn."

Gran began to pace the room like a restless lioness, her eyes sharp and focused. The tie of her worn, floral robe fluttered behind her with each step. "Your mother approves of this plan?"

Cricket's voice was hesitant as she spoke. "I don't think Mama's happy about it." Tikaboo pawed eagerly at Cricket's legs, her big, pleading eyes full of hope. She whimpered softly, her tail wagging furiously. Cricket couldn't resist the adorable sight and bent down to scoop her up into her arms. "Mama's thoughts are consumed by Nadine at the moment."

With a gentle touch, Cricket stepped forward and placed a hand on Gran's arm, halting her anxious pacing. "Did you know Nadine was alive?"

Gran's eyebrows furrowed in confusion and sadness. "Gain one to lose them all," she muttered to herself cryptically, her voice heavy.

Cricket nuzzled her face into Tikaboo's warm fur that was as soft as a cloud, before mustering the courage to ask the question that had been weighing on her mind. "Mama said you orchestrated the disappearance of the crown." Her gaze searched Gran's face for some sign of recognition or remorse, but what she found was an unreadable tapestry of wrinkles and old scars.

Gran's gaze grew steely; she finally stated, "Yes."

Anger simmered and churned deep in Cricket's belly, a rising tide of frustration that threatened to spill over. Why did her family insist on keeping secrets? If Gran and Mama had trusted her and her sisters with the truth from the beginning, they wouldn't be blindsided now. They wouldn't be left floundering, desperately trying to piece together solutions in the eleventh hour. Her voice quivered with intensity as she demanded, "I want to know every single detail about the crown!"

Gran let out an exasperated sigh and rolled her eyes. "So, did Babs pass the challenges and become a member of the summer court?" she asked, steering the conversation toward safer topics.

"More than that," Cricket replied, the image of her sister vivid in her mind. "Babs not only joined the summer court, but she now wears the summer crown and has fangs." She could still recall the blend of awe and fear she felt upon seeing her sister transformed, powerful and fierce.

Gran's face turned as pale as freshly fallen snow at the shocking revelation. The venerable matriarch of the Culebra line took a deep, steadying breath before speaking. "Promise me, child," Gran implored with a voice tinged with both fear and urgency. "Promise me you will never join the winter court." Her eyes, usually filled with wisdom and warmth, now bore an intense, almost desperate plea.

Cricket paused. Gran dreaded the prophecy called "the telling" — predicting that one sister would turn against another, ripping their family apart, with the endless conflicts of the courts destroying even familial ties.

Within Cricket, a tempest churned. To vow never to join the winter court was to renounce a future entwined with Ambrosias. It meant rejecting the winter crown that he yearned to place upon her head — the very crown they were tasked to find. She hesitated, uncertain if she could bring herself to shut that door completely. The draw to Ambrosias was more than a fleeting desire; it resonated with every fiber of her being. Yet the thought of splintering her family and bringing a dark prophecy to fruition left her tentative.

"Gran," Cricket began, her voice wavering between conviction and doubt, "how can I make such a promise when fate seems intent on weaving its threads around me?"

The ground quaked beneath Cricket's feet, a deafening roar reverberating through the air. Cricket shook involuntarily as she gazed on, caught between fear and awe. Reality itself seemed to twist and contort, as if invisible hands were wrenching it apart at the seams. At the heart of this surreal spectacle, a churning vortex of vivid, kaleidoscopic colors burst into existence, its frenetic energy palpable. Trinkets and objects took flight, whirling around the room in a chaotic, mesmerizing dance.

Cricket's heart catapulted into her throat as she beheld the portal's expansion, a breathtaking tear through the very fabric of their world. Emerging from its shimmering maw was Sabella, queen of summer, her blazing mane of hair cascading behind her like an ethereal aurora of flames. The air itself seemed to crackle with intense heat and raw power, pressing down on Cricket like an invisible weight. Sensing imminent danger, her instincts flared to life, and her delicate wings unfurled in a swift motion, propelling her away from potential harm. "Gran!" Cricket cried out, but her voice was swallowed by the sudden maelstrom of arcane energy that surged through the shop, leaving only a whisper in the tempest's wake.

Sabella's eyes, twin orbs ablaze with fiery intensity, locked onto Gran. "Old friend," her voice boomed with authority and power. Her satin gown, a deep shade of crimson, glistened in the dim light of the shop, casting an alluring aura around Sabella. The hem of the dress trailed behind her like a stream of blood, brushing against the ground with each confident step she took. The bodice hugged her curves and accentuated her figure, dipping tantalizingly low and revealing hints of smooth, alabaster skin underneath. Sabella's skin shimmered with a youthful luminescence, casting an otherworldly aura around her. She extended her hand gracefully to Gran, who bowed deeply and pressed a gentle kiss upon it in accordance with tradition. However, a look of visceral disgust flickered across Gran's features, barely veiled by her forced show of respect.

Gran, with her diminutive stature and kind eyes, paled in comparison to the queen's imposing figure. She stood before the queen, questioning her boldly. "You breach my sanctuary, Sabella?" The air around them crackled with tension. Gran's voice trembled slightly, betraying her fear and defiance toward the powerful queen. Despite her small frame, Gran carried herself with a quiet strength that demanded respect.

Sabella moved with the graceful, calculated precision of a predator closing in on its prey. Each barefoot step left fiery imprints on the cool stone floor as she closed in on her target. "This, your sanctuary?" she snarled, her voice dripping with derision and contempt. "You have grown weak, living among these mere mortals, and you have forgotten your rightful place. I have come to remind you and your family of where that place truly is."

Sparks flew as Gran raised her arms, weaving a tapestry of flame to shield herself and Cricket from the impending onslaught. Yet, before the protective barrier could solidify, Sabella unleashed a torrent of fire that splintered it like brittle ice.

The battle that ensued was a cataclysmic dance of destruction. The flames roared and twirled, hungrily devouring the age-old relics and heirlooms that lined the shelves. Gran's magic clashed with Sabella's in sparks and bursts of vibrant colors, each attack and defense more powerful than the last. The air crackled with energy as they circled each other, their eyes locked. With every blow, the room shook and rumbled, threatening to collapse. But neither showed any sign of backing down, their magic raging on like an unstoppable storm.

"Look at you," Sabella taunted, her laughter a horrifying melody amidst the chaos, "old and decrepit. How utterly stupid and wasteful of a life—to fade away here, far from the courts that once revered you."

Cricket's heart raced, overwhelmed by the ferocity of the clash before her. The air crackled with tension as two ancient fire fae clashed, their flames dancing and flickering wildly in a deadly display of power. Desperation surged through her as she longed to leap into the fray, to defend Gran against this formidable opponent. But what damage could her meager air magic do against the raw might of these mythical beings? She felt small and powerless, like a tiny insect caught in the midst of a raging storm. Yet she couldn't shake off the urge to protect her beloved Gran at all costs. Her mind raced, searching for a way to level the playing field in this unequal battle. The smell of smoke and charred earth filled her nostrils. She must find a way to help Gran in any way she could.

Gran's spells grew more frantic, her hands moving in wild, desperate gestures as she defied the summer queen's might. The air crackled with magic and a sense of impending defeat as the shop, once a peaceful haven filled with trinkets and mementos, now lay in ruins around them. Broken shelves and shattered glass littered the floor, casualties of the fierce battle being waged between Gran and the powerful fairy queen. The walls cracked under the onslaught of their magical clash; the building could not withstand their combined forces much longer. Yet Gran's courageousness remained, her wrinkled face contorted in concentration as she fought against the inevitable unraveling of her life in the mortal realm.

"Enough of this!" Sabella bellowed, her voice the harbinger of finality.

Gran, her hair singed and face smeared with soot, stood defiant before Sabella, her body language betraying none of the fatigue that must have crept into her bones.

"You were entrusted with a task, one of vital importance," Sabella hissed. "The crown was to remain hidden, lost to all but the damned gods themselves. You've failed me. You have failed your own line."

Gran's response was a stoic shake of her head, her voice steady as the earth beneath them. "I kept my end of the bargain. That crown is ensconced in shadow and lost to time. It is where no soul would dare seek it. Your reign remains unchallenged, Sabella. I beg you to see reason!"

Cricket floated silently behind a toppled oak armoire, Tikaboo clutched tightly against her chest. Every word they uttered twisted her stomach. Gran had done Sabella's bidding—and seemed to stand by that decision still. The promise of 'the telling'—that prophecy of betrayal and bloodshed—loomed over Cricket, a specter she could neither grasp nor escape.

Sabella's laughter was sharp and cruel, lashing out like whips of flame. "Do you take me for a fool? You, who have chosen to waste away in this . . . this mundane prison, expect me to believe your words?"

With a flick of her wrist, Sabella conjured a searing torrent of fire, an inferno that greedily consumed the very oxygen from the room. Gran raised her trembling hands, a desperate incantation falling from her lips, but the flames were merciless—an unstoppable tidal wave against which her dwindling powers stood little chance.

"Please!" Cricket screamed into the ether, her plea unheard amidst the cacophony of destruction. She darted toward Gran only to be violently hurtled back by the overwhelming force of Sabella's spell, losing her grip on

Tikaboo. As she soared through the air, she could only watch in horror as Tikaboo plummeted to the ground with a sickening thud.

There was a dreadful beauty in the way the fire consumed Gran, the dance of destruction so absolute that it left nothing untouched. In the span of a heartbeat, the woman who had helped raise Cricket, who had taught her the delicate balance between the fae and human worlds, was consumed.

Cricket's scream was lost in the roar of fire, a sound torn from the depths of her being. Her grandmother, her mentor, her anchor to all things gentle and good in the world, was gone. The air around Cricket seemed to still.

"Why?" The word escaped her lips like a broken whisper, fragile and raw. "Why? Why? Why?" Her voice trembled, each repetition growing louder as the weight of her sorrow intensified. "Why? Why? Why?" Desperation seeped into every syllable until she could no longer contain it, wailing, "Why? Why? Why?" The sound was a haunting echo, reverberating through the silence. Her heart shattered into a thousand pieces.

With a slow, tentative limp, Tikaboo hobbled over to Cricket's lap. Her back foot was clearly broken, and she let out a soft whine as her hot tongue licked at Cricket's hand.

As Cricket tenderly caressed her dog's fur, she felt her face contort and crumple. Heart-wrenching sobs convulsed through her chest, sending waves of sorrow that caused tears to stream down her cheeks in hot rivulets.

The queen's fiery aura dimmed now that her purpose was fulfilled. She offered no comfort, no remorse. There was only the cold sterile satisfaction of a queen who had dispatched her version of justice.

Cricket's heart hammered against her chest as the queen turned toward her. The air crackled, charged with the remnants of fire magic.

"Let this be a lesson to you, Cricket of the Culebra line." Sabella's voice was smoldering. "The crown must remain hidden, lost to time and memory. Should you, or any other foolish enough to seek it out, disturb its slumber, you will face losses far more grievous than this."

Terror rooted Cricket to the spot; her breath hitched in her throat. Sabella's warning bore down on her. Without another word, Sabella stepped backward into a swirling vortex that had opened behind her—a rippling tear in reality. It closed with a sound like thunder. Her ultimatum lingered in the destroyed space.

Cricket's legs gave out as she fell to the stone floor, landing in the same spot where Gran had been consumed in fire. "Gran . . ." Her voice cracked and tears streamed down her face without restraint. An overwhelming wave of grief washed over her, clawing at her throat and threatening to engulf her completely. It was a raw, gut-wrenching pain that seemed impossible to bear.

As if responding to the depth of Cricket's sorrow, the air around her began to shimmer. As though countless stars had chosen that moment to descend upon her. They swirled in a dance of cosmic energy, wrapping her in a halo of luminescence. With a sudden burst of brilliance, the cascade of sparks ascended upward. She imagined that each spark carried a piece of Gran's essence, her laughter, her wisdom, her love, lifting them to the heavens where they belonged. Cricket watched, a silent witness to the celestial farewell, the beautiful transformation a stark contrast to the horror that had preceded it.

As the glistening particles grew dim, the room fell dark and still. Awash in awe, Cricket remained transfixed. Silence was all that was left. Gran was gone.

CHAPTER 5

NADINE

Nadine's fingers delicately traced the embossed runes that adorned the weathered cover of Aunt Habina's spell book as she perched on the edge of Babs's bed. The tome, once guarded by Cricket, now lay unexpectedly and boldly upon Babs's desk. How many times had Nadine observed her sisters thumbing through this family heirloom with such ease and familiarity? She had always yearned to touch it, to absorb its wisdom—the collective knowledge painstakingly inscribed by the women of their lineage for future generations. This was all she desired: to be a part of this unbroken chain, passing down their sacred legacy from one generation to the next.

The soft, worn fabric of Babs's favorite sweatpants hugged Nadine's legs like a second skin, providing a comforting warmth against the evening. A borrowed oversized sweatshirt hugged her body like a protective cocoon. Her sock-clad feet curled beneath her as she delved into the ancient pages, each one thick with her family's arcane knowledge. The scent of musty parchment and aged ink filled the small room, transporting Nadine to a secret world of magic and mystery. She ran her fingers over the delicate text, feeling the history imbued within its pages.

The bedroom was bathed in an embrace of comfort—a sanctuary woven from rich earthen tones and sumptuous textures. The warm, earthy scent of Babs filled every nook and cranny of the room. The aroma of freshly cut grass mixed with hints of lavender and musk, creating a unique and inviting fragrance. It was as if nature had been bottled up and poured into the space, providing a sense of calm and grounding to all who entered.

A single lamp on the bedside table cast a golden halo that swaddled Nadine, its warm light sending flickering shadows dancing across the walls. One window allowed the silvery moonlight to cascade into the room, blending seamlessly with the lamplight. The warmth and comfort stood in sharp contrast to the chilly and severe atmosphere of the winter court, which was the only home she had ever known.

Mama's house felt vibrantly alive; it cocooned and cradled its inhabitants in a tender embrace. Nadine could almost feel the house breathe, its welcoming energy wrapping around her like a much needed, comforting hug.

"Seeing you like this, you remind me so much of Babs," Mama said from the doorway, her voice laced with a blend of fondness and a faint trace of something unreadable.

With a gentle, almost reverent touch, Nadine closed the worn book and placed it beside her on the quilted blanket. She looked up at her Mama. The scent of herbal tea and fresh baked bread lingered around her, adding to the sense of calm that radiated from her being. Her face was a canvas of soft curves and open expressions, her large eyes revealing every emotion with unguarded honesty. It was both admirable and frightening—how could someone be so vulnerable and brave at the same time? Nadine wondered how her Mama had managed to keep her heart open after losing her husband to the unpredictable whims of the court. How did she continue to trust and love in a world that had taken so much from her?

"I hope it won't take long for you to see me," Nadine said softly, her words hanging between them like delicate threads waiting to be woven into their relationship. "To know Nadine. Not just as a shadow of Babs."

Mama nodded, a deep pain shimmering in the depths of her brown eyes. Those eyes had weathered countless storms of mourning and endless days of waiting, and now they finally looked upon her long-lost daughter—a stranger sitting before her. The reunion was bittersweet.

Nadine wrestled with a volcano of emotions. She yearned not just to step out from Babs's formidable shadow but to bathe herself in the sunlight of Mama's affection. The notion unfurled within her mind, its tendrils reaching out with an unquenchable thirst.

I will be her most loved. Her favorite, she mused. The thought boldly danced through her consciousness. She could taste a hint of hope. *I will be the daughter she turns to, the one who restores what was torn away.* Each word that echoed in her mind was a spark leaping toward an unseen blaze.

This is how I will make her love me.

Babs has always been the strong one, the leader, Nadine acknowledged. *But now, it is my turn to rise. To claim the love that was denied me, the approval that has hovered just beyond my grasp.*

With an exhale that carried the weight of years spent in icy captivity, she turned to Mama.

"Life at the winter court," Nadine began, her voice measured, "was an unending struggle. Every day was a test of my worth, an endless quest to earn trust." She shifted slightly, her body angling toward Mama as if reaching for a bond that had been fractured before it ever had the chance to solidify. "When my fire magic finally appeared, I was subjected to intense and demanding training. These rigorous sessions shaped my inner resilience. For this, I am truly thankful." She shifted uncomfortably. "Yet no achievement could give me belonging. I remained a prisoner, forever on the fringes."

Mama's brow furrowed deeply, her essence rippling with turmoil in response to Nadine's confession. With concerned grace, she moved closer, the worn wooden floor creaking softly beneath her steps. She sat down beside Nadine on the bed, the mattress sighing and dipping under their combined weight, creating a small valley where they both now shared space and emotion.

"As an outsider, I mastered the art of becoming invisible," Nadine continued, her eyes drifting down to the faded sweatpants that still carried the faint scent of her sister. "I would quietly eavesdrop, melting into the shadows and becoming one with them, absorbing conversations never intended for my ears."

"And?" Mama urged, her voice gentle yet desperate, like the rustle of autumn leaves caught in a brisk wind. "Who stole you from my arms? How did you, an innocent child, become entangled in such a scheme? Your father was seized by the winter court as public retribution, a dire incentive for our family to recover and return the stolen crown. But who took you? And for what purpose? Why let us mourn you as if you were lost forever?"

"Every whisper and shadow of intrigue traces back to Queen Sabella," Nadine murmured, her voice tinged with a blend of fear and resentment as the name slipped from her lips. "She weaves schemes within schemes, an endless web spun into a masterful tapestry."

Mama's hands clenched into tight fists, her knuckles turning a harsh white against the deep fabric of her robe. "That Sabella could betray us so completely, that I never pieced it together!" she hissed, each word dripping with disbelief and anger, coiling around her speech like thorny vines strangling a delicate flower. "To steal you from us— my precious baby girl. We fulfilled our end of the bargain. The crown was hidden just as Sabella commanded, leaving her rule untouchable, uncontested!"

Nadine observed the play of emotions across Mama's face, the lines of grief and outrage etched deeply.

Tentatively, Nadine extended her hand, carefully covering one of Mama's tightly clenched fists. "I will transform this curse into my strength," she vowed. "I've returned, Mama. Your only daughter trained in the courts from birth. I'm strong, and ready to fight for what's ours. I know many secrets. Valuable secrets that we can wield to our advantage."

In that moment, surrounded by the trappings of her sister's life—a life cradled in softness and comfort—Nadine embraced her own identity. The daughter once veiled in shadow now stood ablaze with the radiant light of her own inner fire, her spirit unfurling like a phoenix rising from the ashes. She was ready to claim her place in the world, and within the tender confines of her mother's heart.

Mama's breath hitched, her chest rising and falling rapidly as she moved closer to Nadine on the bed. She perched delicately at the edge. Her eyes were dilated and watery, memory flickering in their depths. "Your father . . ." Mama's voice cracked, struggling to push out the words. She took a shuddering breath before continuing. "Over the years, the druids of Avalon lent me their sight, allowing me to peer across the veil. I saw his form in cursed repose—hidden away in winter's dark night. But you, my sweet Nadine, were veiled from me, hidden by magics that even they could not unravel." A sorrowful sigh escaped her lips as she reached out to gently stroke Nadine's hair.

Nadine felt fire rising within her. "Our family has suffered at the hands of the court's manipulations for far too long. The Culebras are not pawns." She envisioned a plan for achieving victory. "We will no longer bow to the ruling families. That stops tonight." With her energy surging, Nadine could no longer stay seated. "I will lead my sisters in delivering the crown to the winter court as commanded by the winter king, and in doing so, break the chains that bind Father and me to that frozen realm."

Mama pleaded, "What can I do to help?"

Nadine pursed her lips. "You are the heart of our family, and your support gives me strength. Promise me that you have faith in me. Know in your heart that I will achieve this for you. Believe that I will come back to you quickly. With your support, there is nothing I can't accomplish."

"Look at you, my fierce girl," Mama murmured, brushing a loose strand of hair from Nadine's face. "You hold so much strength within you."

"Strength is all I have ever known," she admitted softly. "But it is your love, Mama, that gives it purpose."

Mama reached out, her hand grasping Nadine's. The touch bridged the chasms of time and distance, anchoring Nadine to this singular moment of connection.

"Then let that love be your shield," Mama said, her voice rich with the timbre of the ancient earth. "Let it guide you through the coldest nights and into the light that awaits us on the other side."

Nadine's plea was intense, sounding more like that of a small child than a grown woman. "Please promise me," she begged, "that your love for me will never waver, no matter what happens."

Mama's embrace blanketed Nadine, her words as solid and unwavering as the mountains themselves. "You are Culebra, my dear, and I am yours."

Nadine stiffened and stepped back. Although she yearned for it, she wasn't used to being touched in this way. Mama tilted her head in confusion but soon nodded as comprehension dawned on her. She turned to leave, saying, "Good night then, my dear."

The moonlight was still shining through the curtains, turning everything soft. Nadine walked toward the window and peered out at the large orchard that stretched beyond, her hand resting lightly on her tummy.

A deep breath steadied her racing heart; the air tasted of earth, mingling with the faintest scent of citrus from the groves. Her mind teetered on the edge of tomorrow's chal- lenges, knowing that winning her sisters' trust was pivotal. Each one held a key to the intricate lock that guarded their father's freedom — and her own.

"My sisters," she whispered into the night air, her breath forming a faint mist. "Maybe I can persuade them. Show them that I belong. That they can trust me." She pictured them, each sister wielding their unique and powerful magic, their expressions as resolute as hers. Following her lead.

With nightfall caressing the world outside, Nadine turned back to the bed, her gaze falling on Aunt Habina's spell book. She would spend the rest of the night memorizing its pages, learning its secrets. She knew that knowledge was power, a weapon she wielded with as much skill as her fire magic.

She closed her eyes, allowing her ideal daydream to take shape. She saw the lost crown gleaming in her hand, ready to be given to the winter king, her father released from his chains. Her parents standing together, hands clasped, eyes aglow with the love that had endured decades of separation. Mama's gardens blooming around them, alive with fae magic, and her laughter at the center of their family, reunited at last. The image burned bright, searing itself into her heart.

The cacophony of the kitchen door swinging open from downstairs jolted her out of her daydream. Above the hum of the cicadas outside, she could hear Cricket's fervent voice and then Mama's agonizing wail. The sound of her own rapid footsteps echoed on the wooden stairs as Nadine hurried down to see what was causing all the commotion.

As Nadine crossed into the kitchen, she was met with a startling sight. Cricket stood in the center of the room, covered from head to toe in a layer of ash and soot that clung to her like a second skin. Her clothes were torn and stained, revealing scrapes and bruises on her body that told of a recent fall. In her arms, Tikaboo whimpered softly, clearly shaken by whatever had happened.

Mama's sobs echoed through the room, her cries of disbelief and agony puncturing the stillness. "It can't be!" she wailed, tears streaming down her face. "Gran can't be dead!" Every anguished word seemed to reverberate off the walls, filling the air with a sense of despair and heartache. The weight of loss hung heavy in the room, as if each sob were an anchor dragging them all down into a bottomless sea of grief. Mama's trembling hands reached out for support, grasping at anything to hold on to as she tried to process the impossible truth before her.

Nadine gently led her to a wooden chair at the kitchen table, its surface worn smooth from years of use. The chair creaked softly with familiarity as she settled into it.

Nadine straightened her posture, rolling her shoulders back in a display of confidence and control. Her face remained stoic, betraying no emotion as she addressed Cricket. "Please, begin right from the start," she requested with a calm, measured tone as she turned gracefully to place the teakettle onto the stove. The soft clink of metal against metal echoed briefly in the quiet room, and the gentle hiss of gas igniting accompanied her deliberate movements. Steam began to rise slowly from the spout, curling upward like delicate wisps of smoke, while the warm aroma of brewing tea filled the air.

Nadine observed Cricket ease into the chair across from Mama at the table. Her fingers naturally found their way to the thick, velvety fur of Tikaboo. As Cricket gently stroked his soft coat, Nadine could see her mind wander through a maze of thoughts, slowly arranging them like pieces of an intricate puzzle. The room was filled with quiet expectancy as Cricket prepared to share her story. Nadine carefully placed steaming mugs of tea in front of Mama and Cricket, the savory aroma of matcha wafting through the air. The steam curled upward in delicate tendrils, disappearing into the warm glow of the kitchen light. She then gracefully took her seat next to Cricket.

With her voice hollow and eyes wide with shock, Cricket recounted in a flat, emotionless tone the harrowing tale of how Sabella had coldly ended Gran's life and decimated the family store. She conveyed the chilling warning that retrieving the crown would spell an even graver doom for the

Culebra family. Cricket's voice was filled with anguish as she spoke. "I was utterly useless," she lamented, her words dripping with regret and guilt. "Frozen in fear, I watched helplessly as Gran—" Cricket stopped speaking and rummaged through the front pocket of her hoodie, her fingers brushing against the soft fabric before she finally extracted the diminutive form of Burt.

Nadine's eyes lit up as she saw the tiny gnome perched cross-legged on Cricket's palm. Burt wore a blue hat that flopped endearingly over his right eye, giving him an almost whimsical appearance despite his somber expression. As a duende—a master of the household—Burt's very essence was tied to his home, and it was clear from his downcast face that he did not relish being away from it. The air around him seemed to carry a weight of reluctance, as if each moment outside his familiar surroundings was torture. "I'll take him upstairs with me. He will acclimate to his new surroundings."

"Burt," he whispered, his voice barely more than a breath, repeating the name as if it were a cherished mantra.

"Yes, Burt. I know you well," Nadine replied warmly, her eyes softening as she carefully took him from Cricket's soot-streaked hands. "I will be your Little N. You are going to find so much happiness here."

Burt's cherubic face lit up with excitement, his eyes sparkling like tiny stars as he asked, "You play Find?"

Nadine smiled, "I have played with you before; you just didn't see me. I was hiding."

"Burt did not find," Burt declared, a deep frown creasing his forehead.

Nadine cooed softly, her voice like a gentle breeze through the trees. "No, you couldn't have found me. I was invisible. But I am invisible no longer."

Rubbing at her red eyes, Cricket resumed her tale. "Before leaving, I cast an invisibility spell on the shop. No human or fae can lay eyes upon it now." She gestured; thick shimmering magic swirled and danced in the air around her hands. "But that's not all," she continued. "I also added layers of protection spells on the sub and the door that leads down to it. The space is impenetrable, a fortress of enchantments. Nothing and no one can enter or exit without our knowledge."

"Well done, Cricket," Mama said softly. "We should rest now. The sun will be rising in a few hours." Mama rose from her seat and headed toward the stairs.

"Yes," Nadine agreed. "Let's try to get some rest before we set off tomorrow."

Cricket sprang to her feet, her long legs unfolding like a tall tower. Tikaboo leapt from her lap and tumbled into a tight ball under the table, seeking shelter in the large shadow cast by Gwylm, Babs's great wolf, who slumbered peacefully.

"Set off?" Cricket exclaimed, her voice tinged with disbelief. "But how can we possibly continue on our quest for the crown after everything Sabella has said and done?"

Nadine gently cupped Cricket's tearstained face in her hand, smudging the soot that smeared her cheeks. Nadine's voice was soft and comforting, like a mother soothing a frightened child. "Sister," she whispered, "we will find the crown and free Father. Our family will be reunited. And — when it's all said and done — no one from Inanna's line will ever dare to threaten or harm a Culebra again. I swear this to you."

CHAPTER 6
ZADIE

Zadie ran her hand over the smooth, cool bamboo sheets, reveling in their silky texture. The bed had been freshly made, each fold and crease carefully smoothed out by her own hands. It was a simple pleasure, but one that brought her immense satisfaction.

As her gaze fell upon Tom's pillow, a tight knot formed in her throat, threatening to choke her. But she refused to give in to the overwhelming emotion. Their night together had been nothing short of magical, and she clung to every precious memory. She knew that the bittersweet pain of love lost was far better than never having experienced such intense emotions at all. It was a reminder of how deeply she could feel, and she wouldn't trade that for anything.

Yara's and *Dulcinea's* telepathic whispers danced through Zadie's mind, their soothing words offering a warm embrace. She couldn't hide her true feelings from them, but she didn't want to. Their deep connection brought her solace in this moment of need. As the comforting voices echoed in her thoughts, Zadie felt a sense of gratitude for the bond they shared. It was like a safety net, always there to catch her when she fell.

The clatter of footsteps above broke the rhythmic lapping of water against the hull, announcing the arrival of her sisters.

Zadie's breath hitched as she climbed the small set of stairs that led to the deck. Cricket's eyes were swollen and bloodshot, her cheeks drained of color. It was evident that something had occurred since they'd seen each other last. Zadie's concern grew as she watched her sister struggle to even stand upright.

Zadie did a double take when Nadine appeared beside Cricket. While she shared the same physical features as Babs, her body language was completely different: tense and fidgety, with tightly clenched hands that expressed impatience.

Lastly, Babs strode onto the deck with a quiet presence full of reserve. The summer crown sat proudly upon her head, a dazzling symbol of her new authority. At her side sauntered her ever-present large black wolf, Gwylm. Zadie wondered how the canine would fare at sea.

"Zadie." Babs's voice was unusually measured. "We can't let this stand."

Babs casually tucked a loose strand of hair behind her ear. Gwylm, the lumbering figure, made his way to the front of the ship, his massive shoulders swaying with each step beneath his thick fur coat. *Yara* and *Dulcinea* spoke to him telepathically, their voices ringing in Zadie's mind. Babs tilted her head curiously and grinned. This was new. As far as Zadie was aware, Babs and Gwylm had never heard *Yara's* voice before. Zadie assumed it must be the power from Babs's new crown.

Zadie shifted her gaze between the faces of her three sisters. "Am I missing something?" She placed her hands on her hips.

"Babs," Cricket's soft voice whispered, "she doesn't know. I didn't have a chance to call her." Cricket gracefully took a seat at the back table, crossing her arms and resting her head in their crook.

Zadie shifted her weight from one bare foot to the other. "Can someone please tell me what's going on?"

Nadine walked over to Zadie with a sense of assurance and placed a hand on her waist. "There was an incident at Baubles and Whatnots last night." Nadine looked over her shoulder at Cricket and sighed. "There was an altercation between Queen Sabella and Gran. Cricket witnessed— Your Gran—" Nadine swallowed hard. "Gran didn't have a chance against that kind of power."

Zadie's breaths came in short, sharp gasps, but her lungs still felt empty. Her body was frozen, overcome with a sense of dread and fear that left her unable to move. Everything around her seemed to fade into blocks and pixels as her mind struggled to process the overwhelming sensory input, the telltale signs of a panic attack taking hold. Her mouth felt like it was filled with cotton and glass. "That's not possible."

Cricket rose from her seat and approached Zadie, her hand reaching out but hesitating just before making contact. "Everything feels so fragile," Cricket whispered, her voice trembling. "I don't think we should risk defying Queen Sabella. We shouldn't go after the crown." Cricket's emotions overwhelmed the features of her face, and she let out a sob. "I can't lose anyone else! I can't!" She collapsed into Zadie's arms, losing any semblance of control.

The news of Gran's death sat like a hard jagged stone in Zadie's belly. Cricket's grief only made it grow.

Nadine's fists clenched at her sides, the air around her shimmering with heat as if in symphony with her rising anger. "We can't just abandon our plan. We need that crown—our father's freedom depends on it. My freedom depends on it."

Cricket's hands fluttered to her face, a telltale sign of her distress. "But Sabella's warning was clear," she countered, her voice carrying the weight of concern. "Pursuing the crown could lead us to losing someone else. You weren't there! You didn't see!"

The tension stretched taut between the sisters, their stances rigid upon the wooden deck of *Yara*.

"Father is languishing in the winter court's dungeons because of this," Nadine continued, her silver eyes blazing. "If we turn back now, we betray him and everything Gran sacrificed for us."

Zadie was unsure of the right course of action. The discordant pull of their words were like opposing currents threatening to separate them all.

Cricket argued, her long hair billowing in the sea breeze, "Gran wouldn't want us to walk blindly into danger." She chewed on her bottom lip. "What good is retrieving a crown if we fall prey to Sabella's malice?"

Zadie rubbed at her temples, willing her head to clear. "Both of you have sound judgement," she said, her voice threading between their emotionally charged words. "But we must find a path forward that doesn't abandon our father or cost us someone else we love."

Her words hung there, amidst the scent of salt and the cries of distant gulls. The sisters exchanged tense glances, the decision pressing down upon them like the heavy cloak of an impending storm.

Babs paced the deck slowly, deliberately. "Cricket, you don't have anything to fear from Sabella. None of you need fear." Her voice was flat and devoid of any emotion. If Zadie hadn't been looking at her directly, she might not have recognized the voice as her own sister's. "I'm going to kill her," Babs growled.

Gwylm's head jerked upward, his gaze locking onto Babs as he quickly made his way to her side. His fur bristled as he took a defensive stance. Babs absentmindedly stroked his hide with her fingers. Her brown eyes, normally warm embers, now blazed with an infernal fury. "Gran didn't just fade; she was murdered," she hissed, the air around her growing dense, as if the earth itself were rallying to her wrath. "By all the old gods and all the rulers that came before me, I swear, Sabella will pay for this."

Yara's deck shuddered slightly beneath their feet.

"Vengeance is a dark path," Zadie interjected, the gentle lilt of her voice a drastic contrast to the seething rage that emanated from her sister. "I ache with the same loss, Babs, but Gran's strength was in her level thinking." Zadie stepped closer, her cerulean gaze reflecting both the depth of the ocean they would soon traverse and the tumultuous doubts swirling within her. "We must secure the crown, yes—but let it not be at the cost of fracturing what she held most dear: us, together, as family."

Babs seemed to calm at Zadie's words. Her shoulders relaxed and her eyes softened.

The sails of the *Yara* fluttered, eager to catch the wind and carry them toward their fated destiny.

Nadine's voice was unusually soft as she posed the question, "Are we all in agreement? We must retrieve the crown and rescue Father. Let us honor Gran's memory by remaining united."

Cricket nodded, strands of hair dancing about her face like wisps of thought.

Babs tilted her head from side to side, a smirk spreading across her face in a chilling manner. "We have an accord."

Zadie observed the tension melting from her sisters' faces, their expressions softening. Her fingers traced the weathered lines of *Yara*, her touch tender, as if soothing an old friend's worries. She scanned the deck, seeing the ropes were coiled and stowed, the hatches were secured. She had checked the sails for integrity and ensured the provisions secured in their holds.

Zadie took command and confidently announced, "We set sail." *Yara* shivered in response as they smoothly left the marina and headed out into the crystal-clear water. The sky above was a wash of pastel hues, with thick peach and pink clouds hovering just above the horizon. The early sun peeked through the gaps, casting a warm golden glow.

"Zadie?" Cricket's voice was hard to hear over the wind. "I just wanted to make sure you were all right. I'm sorry I didn't call."

The water that stretched out before them reflected the clouds and the light that danced on its surface, as if they had sailed into a Maxfield Parrish painting.

"I'm fine. It's fine," Zadie said, rallying her own courage as much as bolstering her sisters'. She wrapped her arm around Cricket's waist. Zadie allowed herself a final glance back at the shore, at the life she was leaving behind. The taste of salt on her lips wasn't just from the ocean breeze; it was the bittersweet flavor of sacrifice and the sting of responsibility.

The spray of the sea whispered secrets as *Yara* and *Dulcinea* exchanged thoughts that rippled through the timbers of the ship. "*Sisters of land*," murmured *Yara*, her consciousness melding with the creak of the deck, "*their ties fray like weather-worn rope.*"

"*Indeed.*" *Dulcinea's* essence hummed along the mast. "*The winds foretell a tempest within as much as without.*" The ship, with its sentient guardians at the helm, sensed the undercurrents of discord among the sisters, the silent tremors of conflict that threatened to erupt.

Zadie overheard the conversation held in whispers of magic between the mastheads as they focused on the horizon. She felt the vessel respond to the soothing waves, eager to prove her worth on the open sea.

"Steady," Zadie said as much to herself as to them. "Let's catch the wind," Zadie commanded, her tone steady. With the precision born of countless voyages, the sisters released the sails, unfurling them fully with reverence for the journey ahead. The white canvas blossomed against the blue backdrop, drinking in the gusts that swept in from the open ocean.

As *Yara* glided past the last buoy marking the safety of the marina, a pod of dolphins appeared in the water beside her. Their sleek bodies danced through the waves, their joyful clicks and whistles echoing in perfect harmony. The sun glinted off their smooth skin, creating a sparkling display. Their playful swim added a touch of levity to the moment. The boat cut a path through cobalt waters, leaving a frothy wake to mark where the world of order ended and the realm of chaos began.

Zadie moved to the helm, her grip on the wheel an anchor against the swell of emotions that threatened to capsize her. The sea stretched before them, a canvas painted with the hues of their destiny — deep and fathomless.

With each mile *Yara* claimed from the shore, Zadie felt the tendrils of the human world — of Tom and his earth-bound love — slipping like sand through her fingers. Yet the call of her Mer lineage surged within her, an ancient melody harmonizing with the siren song of adventure. As the coastline faded into a whisper of land, Zadie's vision blurred. She blinked the tears away.

"Troubled waters ahead," Dulcinea's voice whispered through the creak of wood and rope, a portent wrapped in the guise of the elements.

And though none spoke it aloud, the air thrummed with the understanding that Sabella's shadow, cast long and ominous, was but the first of many threats they would face. The crown, an artifact steeped in power and peril, beckoned them forward.

As *Yara* disappeared into the embrace of the open sea, Zadie felt the finality of the moment settle around her. There was no turning back now. Her journey had begun.

CHAPTER 7

BABS

Babs bent down, sorting through the jumbled stack of canned goods in the cubby as Gwylm sat resting at her feet. Each can was missing its label, but the contents were written on the lid in neat black marker. She couldn't understand why Zadie would do this. Back at Mama's house, they had beautifully crafted glass jars with handwritten labels clearly marking the fruits and vegetables that had been grown the previous season. It was quite an ordeal, harvesting and canning, but there was such a satisfying rhythm to the task. It was so rewarding to gaze on the pantry when it was full and orderly. Babs made a mental note to improve her sister's pantry organization—and contents. This wasn't living; it was just getting by.

The voices inside her head buzzed like a swarm of busy bees, a constant hum that separated her from the world around her. When Liande had asked her to steal the crown, it had seemed like the only option—a necessary task for their victory. It had felt right at the time, in that moment; it had felt exhilarating and satisfying. A thrill unlike anything she had ever experienced. But as the morning sun illuminated everything around her and she stood in the hull of Zadie's boat, she felt ill at ease. Babs was second-guessing herself.

Looking back, it was as if she had been under a spell. Maybe it was the strain of trying to get Cricket to smile after the dreadful breakup with Bash. Or the stress of Nadine showing up in such a cantankerous, combative way. Or perhaps it was the influence of all the conflicting voices inside her head. Or the ache she buried deep down inside herself, grief from losing Gran.

Gwylm's low voice floated into her mind. *"Your agitation is upsetting."*

She responded out loud, "I'm sorry. I'll try to keep it under control."

He inquired further. *"Is it the ocean? Being far from land? Run your hands through my fur. It will calm you."*

Her voice was a small whisper. "Gran." A hot tear threatened to spill from her eyes. She would not think about that. She went straight to rage when she thought of what Sabella had done. Rage. She couldn't wait to dethrone her.

Gwylm shifted his weight, apparently noticing the change in her energy as she forcefully sorted the ugly tin cans. *"Are you going to inform me of your plans? With you, there is always a plan within a plan."*

She realized if she delivered the crown to Liande, it most likely would doom her father to eternal captivity. How had she not seen that before?

"Gwylm, we serve the summer court. What is best for the court comes before all else, even if there are sacrifices to be made. Personal sacrifices. Right?"

The whispers of the crown heightened, luring her thinking into a murky dark puddle. *"You have the strength to rule, Babs. Don't let anyone stand in your way. Whether your sisters give the crown to the king, or Liande does, it matters not."*

The voices quieted as Gwylm's voice came to the forefront. *"As with all things, follow your heart."*

Her main concern was putting an end to Queen Sabella. Was this a result of listening to her heart, or was it fueled by hate?

Gaining the support of the winter court would make ruling alongside Liande much easier. However, this could only be achieved if she gave Liande the crown to present to the winter king. Was ambition guiding her decision, or was it her rational mind instead of her emotions?

Her fingers tightened around a can of peaches as she fought to find her own thoughts through the cacophony of noise inside her head. Her heart raced with the exertion, leaving her breath jagged and labored.

"As always, you have given me pause, Gwylm."

As if responding to her inner turmoil, the mark on her arm began to glow — a vibrant gold that pulsed with every beat of her heart. It was the symbol of her connection to Liande, a constant reminder of their pledge to each other.

Liande, Babs thought, reaching out telepathically. *I'm so confused.*

"You are on a straight path," came the response, melodic and warm like the earth after a summer rain. *"I see in the pool our success. Fear not."*

Liande was tranced, Babs thought. She spoke the possible futures.

"Gran . . . Gran's dead," Babs choked out, the words tasting bitter in her mouth. "Sabella killed her."

"Vengeance is a powerful motivator," Liande mused. *"Your desire for justice is understandable. Use that fire in your belly to find the crown."*

"If I give you the crown, the winter king will have no

reason to free my father. Nadine was tasked to find it as well." Babs's voice trembled with emotion.

"Timing must be of the utmost importance if the king is send-ing many for the crown." Liande's voice clamored in Babs's mind over the others. *"Sometimes, sacrifices must be made for the greater good,"* Liande replied. *"But I promise you this, Babs: If you deliver unto me the crown and help me overthrow Sabella, you will have the power and freedom to do as you will."*

Babs shut the cubby door and secured it with the latch. The cans were now slightly more organized, but her mind felt overcrowded. Her thoughts were unconnected, dis-jointed.

"When you are queen and Sabella is dead" — Babs's shoulders straightened, her resolve hardening like a rough, uncut diamond — "I will use my influence to free my father."

There was no response from Liande, and the mark on Babs's arm pulsed once more before fading back to its usual hue. A sense of purpose settled over her, as though a storm had passed and left behind a quiet strength.

Gwylm's voice came into her mind. *"Plans within plans."*

She donned a heavy yellow foul-weather jacket, pants, and boots that Zadie insisted they all wear when above deck. Gwylm's massive form maxed out his jacket.

"Gwylm, I will find a way to accomplish everything I desire. I will seek justice for Gran's death. Sabella will be overthrown. Nadine and Papa will return to Mama. And I will reign alongside Liande."

His voice was solemn. *"I will be by your side, every step of the way."*

She awkwardly climbed the few steps up and took a mo-ment to steady her stance, Gwylm right behind her. Dark clouds gathered ominously above the vessel as they sailed deeper into the blue waters. Thunder rumbled in the distance, echoing across the churning waters like the growls of a furious beast. Lightning streaked through the skies, illuminating the tempestuous waves that rocked the boat, making Babs stomach queasy. She was handling being in the open water better than she ever had been. Perhaps the power of the crown upon her head was giving her strength. She laid her hand upon Gwylm.

"Zadie," Cricket called out, her voice barely audible over the roar of the wind, "why is this storm so violent?"

Zadie's bearing was steady, even in the turbulent sea. Her eyes were filled with a mix of awe and excitement as she gazed at the towering waves. "The Bermuda Triangle is a place where the veil between our world and Atlantis is thin," she explained, raising her voice to be heard. "It causes storms and other anomalies on this plane."

Nadine gripped the ship's railing tightly, her normally rosy complexion turning a sickly shade of green. "What sort of abnormalities?" she asked, her frown deepening.

Zadie spoke with hushed reverence, her words carrying the weight of ancient secrets. "Hidden deep beneath the waves, at the very heart of Atlantis, rests a grand pyramid known as the Hall of Time." She paused to tighten a line. "For centuries, this pyramid has stood as the epicenter of all time manipulation in Atlantis. Above it, an inverted invisible pyramid hovers in midair, its presence both ominous and mysterious. Beware, for any who venture too close may find themselves trapped in a timeless limbo, their existence suspended between past and present."

Nadine's expression turned sour as she absorbed Zadie's words. "So it's not a triangle, it's actually an invisible upside-down pyramid. And we're headed straight toward it!"

Zadie untangled a twisted line in the gusty wind. "As below, so above."

Babs furrowed her brow. "Don't you have that saying backward?"

Zadie replied with a coy smile. "Do I?"

The weight of Zadie's words hung heavy in the air as Babs's heart pounded in unison with the intensifying storm. The sea churned around them, each wave crashing against the boat with a deafening roar and drenching them in icy saltwater spray. The thunder and lightning raged on, illuminating the dark sky with jagged bolts of light.

Babs was no stranger to the mystical fairylands, but she had never imagined venturing into the treacherous underwater world of the Mer. The very thought made her stomach twist with unease. Were they even allowed? As if in warning, the raging waves seemed to taunt and challenge her to enter their realm. But as they pressed forward toward their inevitable crossing, queasiness and fear overtook her.

Zadie, with urgency in her voice, urged *Yara* to reef the sails. As *Yara* responded by lowering the sails halfway, Zadie scanned the horizon and homed in on the impending wall of dark water they were heading toward.

The deck of the ship was slick with seawater, causing the girls' boots to slip and slide as the ship violently pitched, rolled, and yawed like a wild animal. They flailed their arms, desperately grasping for anything to hold on to as they were thrown around like dice in a game of chance. The wood beneath them seemed to groan and creak under the strain of the storm. Their bodies were jolted and twisted in every direction, leaving them bruised and battered by the relentless force of the sea.

"I'm sorry!" Zadie shouted. "Our destination is in the direction of the wind. It's going to be a violent crossing.

Make sure you secure yourselves with the harnesses!" She gestured toward the tethers and clipped herself in. "That way, if the wind knocks you off your feet, you won't go overboard."

Babs's fingers were numb and wrinkled from the frigid ocean water as she grabbed the clips on her harness and secured them tightly to a midpoint hook for both herself and Gwylm.

Zadie gestured toward the bright red cord attached to her jacket. "If you do happen to get swept out to sea, pull this and it will inflate. The beacon will notify me of your location."

Cold, clammy sweat coated Babs's skin as her imagination ran wild with the terrifying possibility of being lost at sea. She could almost feel the icy water engulfing her body, the slimy tendrils of sea creatures wrapping around her limbs, and the crushing weight of the deep ocean pressing in on her. The deluge of salty spray was relentless against her face as she gripped onto the harness line for dear life.

Gwylm's voice urged in Babs's mind. "*Stay calm.*"

Their destination seemed to warp and twist before Babs's eyes as they ventured deeper into its treacherous waters. The storm had not abated, but now it was accompanied by an unsettling sense of disorientation. Time itself appeared to be bending around them, causing their surroundings to shift and change in bewildering ways.

"Look!" Cricket cried out, pointing toward the horizon. A massive pirate ship loomed in the distance, cannons blazing as it exchanged fire with a rival vessel. The fabric of their sails was aged and rough, beaten by years of exposure to the salty sea air. The thick canvas looked like old leather.

Each billowing crease seemed to ripple and pulse, almost like a living creature trying to break free from its confines. The holes scattered across the sails were like open wounds, flapping and tearing in the relentless wind.

"Is that a mirage?" Babs wondered aloud, her voice soft with astonishment as she gripped the lifeline.

"It's like a ride at Disney!" exclaimed Cricket, her face alight with wonder. "Can you believe it?"

As the pirate ships vanished behind a curtain of rain, another scene unfolded before them: a World War II–era sparkle ship, its hull gleaming with patches of black and white. The swirling patterns on its surface seemed to change with every passing moment, almost like a kaleidoscope shifting and twisting. Fighter planes zoomed overhead, their metal bodies reflecting the lightning in blinding flashes. The sound of their engines roared through the air, drowning out the crashing waves and the distant rumble of thunder. Gunfire erupted from their tails, sending bursts of bright sparks toward the pirate ship in the distance. The scene was chaotic and yet mesmerizing, a fusion of past and present colliding in a whirlwind of colors and sounds.

Nadine whispered, her eyes wide with awe and terror, "What is happening?"

"Time is collapsing in on itself," Zadie explained, her words barely audible above the din of battle. "We must navigate through this chaos and reach the sunken pyramid before we become lost in time ourselves."

Babs gritted her teeth against the onslaught of chaos, her hands trembling as she fought to maintain control.

"Stay with us, Babs," Cricket implored, while reaching out to grab her hand. "I know you're afraid of the ocean. But trust Zadie; she'll get us through this."

"Starboard!" Zadie shouted, drawing the others' attention back to their surroundings. They'd sailed into a maelstrom of chaos, where zeppelins and planes clashed overhead like titanic beasts of legend.

Babs swore, her voice wavering between fear and despair. When would this end?

Zadie, her eyes wild as the sea, began to sing her Mer song. Her siren's song was both enchanting and mournful. Her words carried a sense of longing and desperation, seeping into every crevice and echoing through the chaos. It was a haunting melody that called to the ancient powers of the sea, their response rumbling in the depths and stirring the currents. Each note cut through the chaos like a beacon of hope, pulling them toward their destination. Tears streamed down her face as she sang, her voice trembling with deep emotion. "Please, Atlantis," she pleaded in between verses. "We desperately need your help!"

"Zadie, keep singing!" Babs shouted over the cacophony. "We have to believe that they will hear us!"

"Does it end before it begins?" Nadine questioned, her voice barely audible over the raging storm. "Are we to be lost at sea, caught between worlds?" She turned away while emptying the contents of her stomach on the ship's hull.

Zadie's voice was a lifeline, cutting through the chaos and holding them together like a strong rope. Each note she sang was like a hand reaching out, grasping at something solid in the midst of the storm. And in that moment, as the winds howled and the waves roared, all they could do was hold on to each other and trust in the magic of the sea to guide them to safety. Zadie's voice never faltered, her connection to the ancient power growing stronger with each word she sang.

"Atlantis, please!" Zadie cried out once more, her plea rising above the storm.

Their pale faces were slick with rain and fear, their knuckles white as they clung to the sides of the boat. Babs felt especially stricken. "Zadie," she murmured, her voice wavering as much as her sister's song. "I can't stand being on the water like this for much longer."

Zadie faltered for a moment, her crazed eyes locking on Babs. Her voice came out in ragged gasps. "Hold on. I'll keep singing. We'll make it through."

Babs clenched her teeth, willing herself to push aside her fear. She hated weakness, especially in herself.

As Zadie's siren song rose to a powerful crescendo, lightning tore through the sky. It illuminated a colonial-era warship that sailed alongside them for a brief, surreal moment. The sisters exchanged wide-eyed glances as the ship vanished in a swirl of wind and waves. Time seemed to fracture around them, offering fleeting glimpses of history's secrets.

"Did you see that?" Cricket gasped, her eyes shining with awe despite the peril of their situation.

Yet even as she spoke, the tempest briefly abated, revealing a swirling disk soaring high above. Its shape was sleek and streamlined, almost like a flying saucer from a science fiction movie. It glided through the air, weightless and effortless, defying the strong winds and turbulent waves below. Zadie's eyes locked on it, mesmerized by its beauty and mystery. As the storm engulfed it once again, it disappeared from sight, leaving behind a sense of wonder and curiosity in its wake.

"Is this . . . time travel?" Nadine asked, her voice quivering with wonder and fascination.

Zadie replied, "Something like that." Her melodic voice strained as she sang her Mer song.

As the storm intensified, the waves becoming mountainous walls of water, Zadie's siren song grew desperate, reaching out to the Mer for salvation.

Her voice was a lifeline for Babs as she tried to block out the visions of pirate battles and flaming zeppelins.

Zadie pleaded, "Please, Mer, hear my song!"

Babs knew that if they didn't receive help soon, they would be lost forever in the chaotic maelstrom of time and sea.

Nadine shouted, "Zadie, look!" pointing to a shimmering figure emerging from the depths below: a mermaid, her intense stare iridescent beneath the stormy sky. More Merfolk joined the first. "They're coming to help us!" she cried, pointing at the approaching Mer.

"Quick!" Babs urged, her heart pounding. "We need to prepare for their arrival!"

Just as the words left her lips, a massive wave reared up before them, blocking out the sky and casting a dark shadow over the ship. The sisters looked on in horror as the colossal wall of water loomed overhead, threatening to crush them beneath its immense weight.

"Zadie!" Cricket called out, her voice shaking with terror.

Babs caught a glimpse of the majestic Mer as they emerged from the depths, answering Zadie's call. But before she could fully take in their beauty, they disappeared beneath the tumultuous waves.

In that split second, it felt as though the laws of nature had been suspended. Babs was flung, her body tossed carelessly by the wind and sea. The tether, once a lifeline connecting her to the ship, now felt like a suffocating umbilical cord holding her back from life. As she plummeted into the water below, everything became a blur—the world turned upside down, her breath released all at once in tiny bubbles, and the rush of water filled her ears. Desperately, Babs fought against her restraints, struggling to break free. Then all went black.

CHAPTER 8

CRICKET

Cricket's face was submerged in the cold water, bubbles escaping her lips with each exhale. Her clothes were heavy, pulling her down as she struggled against the powerful current. Her hands clumsily fumbled with the front of her coat, desperately searching for the red pull cord of her safety vest. Tossed around like a lifeless doll in the rough waves, she finally broke through the water's surface. Cold air seared her lungs; her body shivered in shock.

With no respite, towering waves crashed over her head yet again, swallowing her whole. She thrashed about, gasping for air as cold water filled her mouth and stung her nose. Her hands clawed at the surface, desperate for something to hold on to. But all she could see was the capsized ship, *Yara*, sinking deeper into the dark depths far beyond her reach. Her sisters' bright yellow jackets were nowhere in sight, lost in the chaos of the stormy waters. With no sign of rescue in sight, dread washed over her as she realized they were all going to drown.

Perhaps she should give in to the inevitable. She willed her body to relax. Stop struggling. Stop fighting.

Blinding bolts of lightning tore through the darkening sky, throwing the destruction into somber relief. Each flash was like a strobe light, further disorienting her as she floated through the chaos. Thunder crashed and rolled. Electricity permeated the air, pulsing with a chaotic power. With each strike, new details of the devastation were revealed — debris strewn about like leaves beneath a tree in autumn.

The sea roared, a leviathan awakened, its waves towering and toppling with the ferocity of the tempest. The air fae within Cricket recoiled, her instincts screaming for the safety of the skies, yet knowing there was no refuge to be found above or below.

Zadie's voice was like a sharp knife cutting through the chaos. Her urgent tone, not heard but felt, was unmistakable to Cricket. She frantically searched for her sister's whereabouts.

A smooth and sinewy arm, wrapped around Cricket's side. Startled, she turned to find a surprising sight — it wasn't her sister that swam beside her but a magnificent mermaid. Her shimmering scales caught the tumultuous light of the storm, reflecting it in all directions like a prism. Each one glinted and gleamed with a different hue, from deep emerald to pale silver, creating a mesmerizing display of color. The Mer's eyes were a deep blue, reminiscent of the ocean depths, yet they conveyed an aura of serenity and calmness. Her full lips were a striking contrast against her pale skin, their rosy hue resembling the soft petals of a delicate flower. Despite the raging waters around them, she moved with graceful ease.

A beacon of hope emerged from the churning abyss of the ocean — a submarine. Its exterior was an entrancing blend of elegant curves and precise angles, a masterpiece of design. The metallic surface shimmered with bioluminescent colors, casting an eerie glow that danced like ghostly fireflies in the dark water. As it broke free from the turbulent waves, it seemed to glide with an almost supernatural grace, untouched by the surrounding chaos. Its design was unlike anything Cricket had ever encountered. The streamlined, compact form hinted at astounding speed and agility. It resembled a creature born of the deep sea, perfectly evolved to navigate through even the most perilous waters with ease and precision.

The hatch swung open with a creak, revealing beings as majestic as they were enigmatic — two towering, muscular male figures draped in gleaming bronze armor that seemed to absorb the light around them. Their faces were concealed by intricately designed helmets adorned with swirling patterns and mysterious runes, adding an air of impenetrable mystery. Cricket was taken aback to see that they had legs, not the fins she had expected from creatures of the sea like the mermaid holding her. Did these beings possess the ability to transform even beneath the ocean's depths? With fluid grace and undeniable strength, one soldier emerged from the hatch, his movements almost ethereal. He reached out toward her, arms extended wide in a gesture that was both inviting and authoritative. His eyes, shimmering with the very essence of the ocean, held a depth and tranquility that was at once comforting and profoundly loving, like gazing into the heart of the sea itself.

Cricket's eyes darted over the tumultuous waters, her heart pounding as she took in the scene. She spotted other Mers skillfully navigating the churning waves, guiding Nadine and Babs toward the waiting vessel. The sisters were carefully shepherded into the sturdy, metallic haven that remained still amidst the swirling chaos of the stormy sea.

Cricket gasped for breath, her chest heaving as frantic hands peeled away her waterlogged outer clothing. An oversized warm white blanket was swiftly draped over her trembling frame, and the heat began to seep into her frigid limbs, thawing her icy skin. "Where's Zadie?" she stammered through chattering teeth, her voice barely audible over the sound of her teeth chattering. Her eyes darted around the chaotic scene. Babs and Nadine were also swathed in thick towels, their faces pale but relieved under the layers of warmth that cocooned them.

Gwylm plopped himself down on top of Babs's feet, his weight causing her to shift uncomfortably. His fur was drenched from the violent storm outside and emitted an overpowering odor that permeated the cramped space. The musty smell seemed to stick to every surface and object, impossible to escape. Despite the unusual situation, Gwylm seemed at ease as he took his post as guardian. Babs placed her hand gently on his large back, seeming to find comfort in his presence.

Nadine's trembling hand clutched the rim of a weathered bucket as she retched violently, her body convulsing with each agonizing heave. Cricket rushed to her side, gently gathering Nadine's hair and pulling it away from her face, the strands shimmering like embers in the dim light. The dry heaves racked Nadine's slender frame, leaving her gasping for breath between each gut-wrenching spasm. As a fire fae, accustomed to the warmth and vitality of flames, the harrowing experience of nearly drowning must have been an even greater torment, Cricket mused, her heart aching with sympathy for her sister.

The interior of the submarine was unlike anything Cricket had ever encountered—its walls were crafted from a transparent material, offering an unobstructed view of the vast ocean that enclosed them on all sides. It felt as though they were ensconced within a gigantic glass bubble, rather than confined within a metal vessel. Through the crystal-clear barriers, glimpses of vibrantly hued fish and other marine life danced by, their movements fluid and mesmerizing like an underwater ballet. The water remained pristine up to about twenty feet below, where it gradually dissolved into a deep, impenetrable darkness.

Despite the seemingly fragile appearance of the walls, Cricket felt reassured by the robust structure encasing them. She stepped gingerly on the see-through floor, testing its resilience and finding it unwaveringly solid and secure beneath her feet. A gentle hum resonated in her ears as she gazed out into the boundless underwater world that stretched endlessly around them. A serene blend of tranquility and mystery captivated her every sense.

The soldier who had kindly helped her aboard the transport ship removed his helmet, revealing a friendly face with bright eyes and a charming grin. Cricket's heart fluttered at the sight, as if the floor had suddenly dropped out from beneath her. She closed her eyes, focusing on the wave of happiness that washed over her. All her fears and doubts vanished in an instant, replaced by a sense of pure joy and contentment. It was as if she was floating on a warm breeze, surrounded by the sweet scents of summer. "Welcome aboard, Landling," the soldier greeted her warmly. "I presume Zadie is your Mer friend?"

Cricket parted her lips to reveal the truth about Zadie being her sister, but only a series of faint squeaks managed to slip out. The soldier's eyes shimmered like distant stars, mesmerizing her and muddling her thoughts. Her feeble effort to resist his soothing presence only deepened the curve of his smile. Zadie possessed an uncanny talent for weaving this enchantment, casting a serene and affectionate aura over all who surrounded her. Cricket had never truly pondered what it might be like to find herself amidst numerous Mers endowed with Zadie's extraordinary abilities.

He flashed a charming smile, his long fingers expertly brushing a dark strand of hair out of his sparkling eyes. "Your friend is sure to join us later," he informed her smoothly, the warmth in his voice tickling Cricket's ears. He exuded an air of confidence and charm, leaving no doubt that he was used to getting what he wanted.

Babs's voice thundered from behind Cricket. "We aren't going anywhere without our sister Zadie! She could die out there in that ridiculous storm!"

The soldier threw his head back, his laughter erupting like the roar of crashing waves. "Ashur, she actually thinks Merfolk can be taken down by a stormy sea! I told you, Landlings don't know a thing!" His laughter echoed through the ship like the barks of playful seals.

The soldier at the helm ran his calloused fingers through his thick black mane as he turned to face the group. His eyes, smoldering with intensity, raked over Cricket's nervously shifting form. "Enough," he commanded in a deep, authoritative voice. He cast a stern gaze toward the other soldier, quelling any further insults toward their guests. "These are Maj's nieces and Zadie's sisters." He then turned back to Cricket, adopting a gentler tone. "Zadie is currently receiving assistance from your aunt and others to repair her ship. You will have the chance to see her soon enough." The soldier's words were like a calming balm on Cricket's nerves.

With a sharp hiss, the heavy hatch slammed shut, and the tumultuous noise of the raging storm was instantly muted. In its place, Cricket was submerged in a soothing hum of machinery, drowning out the chaos outside. As the submarine began its descent into the depths of the ocean, a deep and ominous rumbling filled the tiny vessel, causing Cricket's body to shudder and her stomach to churn with nerves. The subtle whirring of advanced technology harmonized with the haunting melodies of unseen creatures lurking in the dark waters, creating an otherworldly symphony. Cricket's head began to spin, her thoughts racing and tangling like a messy ball of yarn as she tried to comprehend the incredible rescue she had just experienced.

Her voice was barely a whisper as she managed to utter a heartfelt thank-you, her gaze fixated on Daimon's formidable figure. The words felt small and insignificant compared to the immense gratitude she felt toward the Mers who had saved her from the relentless waves. She had been on the verge of surrendering to the ocean's fury, but they had pulled her back to safety.

Daimon beamed at her with a smile, his eyes crinkling at the corners. A mischievous glint danced in his gaze, revealing his warm nature. His lips curved up into a grin as he gave her a playful wink before turning to assist Ashur with a friendly pat on the back.

As the submarine delved deeper into the ocean's embrace, Cricket's mind whirled with what lay ahead. The storm had been but one obstacle; the true trial still awaited. But in this moment of reprieve, she allowed herself a fleeting respite from the weight of the task before them.

The submarine's interior was draped in an otherworldly glow, casting eerie shadows that danced and flickered across Ashur's gleaming bronze armor. He moved with the practiced grace of a seasoned helmsman, each movement deliberate and controlled. His eyes, a striking shade of seafoam blue, scanned the myriad marine creatures that swarmed around the vessel. Their movements reflected in his gaze, revealing the depth of experience etched into every line of his weathered face — a testament to a lifetime spent navigating the mysteries of the deep ocean.

"Fasten yourselves tightly," Daimon smiled, motioning toward the freshly materialized seats in the heart of the vessel. "We're about to plunge into the depths." His voice carried a calm assurance that seemed almost surreal given the peril that had engulfed them mere moments ago.

Cricket's hand trembled as she clung to the smooth, pearl-like edges of the seat. Her fingers gripped tightly, white-knuckled, as the submarine jolted and swayed through the unforgiving depths of the ocean. Nadine's hand, warm and steady, intertwined with hers, offering a small sense of security amidst the chaos that surrounded them. Together they rode out the turbulent waves and twirls of sea creatures, their movements unpredictable yet graceful. Cricket's eyes widened in wonder as the transparent walls of the vessel provided a dizzying view of the underwater world, filled with vibrant colors and intriguing creatures she had only read about in books.

Observing her wide-eyed reaction, Ashur hesitated before speaking. "The sea creatures only grow more colossal the deeper we venture," he remarked, his voice tinged with a mix of gravity and seriousness.

"No worries back there. We've got you," Daimon teased.

The submarine's hull emitted a deep, mournful groan, a somber melody entwined with the chaos of the time storm raging outside. Inside its metal cocoon, the sisters huddled together, their faces pale and ghostly in the dim, bioluminescent glow that seeped through the vessel's interior.

"Are you doing okay?" Cricket's voice was a soft whisper, intended solely for Babs's ears.

Babs closed her eyes, taking in a deep breath before exhaling slowly. "It's good to face your fears, right?" she replied, her voice tinged with apprehension as her face turned a ghastly shade of green. Gwylm nuzzled her side.

Nadine guarded her thoughts closely, her expression revealing nothing. Daimon's face, chiseled and composed, bore an open beauty as he observed the sisters in their hushed whispers. Cricket could almost glimpse the flicker of thoughts dancing behind his eyes. "It's unprecedented for landlings to be granted passage to Atlantis," he stated, his voice resonating with mischief.

Ashur's voice was low and muffled as he spoke. "If it wasn't for Maj—" His words were cut off by the sharp intake of breath from Babs.

She bristled at his insinuation, her eyes flashing with anger. "We were given a task, one that we fully intend to carry out. It is not your place to question or interfere."

Daimon erupted into laughter, doubling over in hysterics. "Oh yes, the landling has it all figured out," he managed to choke out between wheezing gasps. Tears streamed down his face as he struggled to contain himself. "So much happens in Atlantis that we have no knowledge of, right, brother?"

Nadine sat with her arms tightly folded across her chest, chin jutting out defiantly as if daring anyone to challenge her. Cricket sensed that their behavior was far from the expected decorum of this underwater realm. The subtleties and nuances of etiquette here were a mystery to her, like trying to navigate a labyrinth without a map. If only Zadie were present; her profound knowledge of both terrestrial and aquatic customs would surely help bridge this daunting gap.

It was Ashur who finally took pity on their bewilderment — his expression a mesmerizing blend of dignity and profound honor. "My brother Daimon and I," he began, his voice echoing with an ancient resonance, "are the sons of Tiamat, the last of the majestic water-dragons."

Cricket thought that title seemed incredibly grand. Tiamat — yes, she had heard that name whispered in hushed tones before, but the honorific "water-dragon" was entirely new to her.

Daimon's eyes danced, as he held his arms out wide as if to hug the world. "Our sacred duty is to safeguard the tables of destiny," he began, his sea-glass eyes reflecting mischievousness. "They rest within our hearts and at the heart of our temple, where timelines are conceived and extinguished. This is the sole charge entrusted to Atlantis."

Ashur let out an exasperated sigh, rolling his eyes in frustration. "Daimon," he interjected, "these strangers cannot be trusted with our secrets. Rashly revealing them could have dire consequences."

Daimon straightened his shoulders, ignoring Ashur's concerns. Turning back to Cricket, he concluded, "We will speak further when you are united with your sister."

Ashur motioned for Daimon to join him at the front of the vessel.

As the craft descended deep into the inky abyss, the thrumming of its engines merged with the murmur of the ocean, a symphony that seemed to herald their arrival. The darkness of the deep began to recede, replaced by an ambient glow that grew steadily brighter until it illuminated an underwater city in its entirety.

Cricket's breath caught in her throat at the breathtaking sight of Atlantis — this was no mere myth but a vibrant, resplendent metropolis encased within an immense, shimmering bubble-like dome. The city glowed with ethereal light, its towers and spires reaching toward the surface like fingers of crystal. She stole a quick glance at Babs and Nadine; their faces were illuminated with pure joy and wonder, eyes wide and mouths slightly agape as they took in the awe-inspiring vista before them.

A beautiful amalgamation of past and future, the structures below seemed to defy gravity. Golden pyramids with tips of silver stood side by side with sleek, spiraling spires that reached toward the dome's zenith. Mer creatures, with shimmering iridescent scales, swam gracefully around the perimeter, their powerful tails propelling them effortlessly through the water. As they entered the dome, their forms shifted, morphing into bipedal beings as they joined the bustling crowd walking the city's gilded streets. Cricket marveled at the dome's enchantment, allowing only the Mer to pass through its invisible barrier as if it were made of wispy smoke.

As the submarine approached, an imposing line of titans stood guard at the entrance, each one a towering figure sculpted from the very depths of the sea. Their vigilant eyes scanned the vessel as it drew near, granting passage only when satisfied that there was no threat. A bustling array of futuristic seacraft came into view, moving in and out of the city with a dizzying display of orchestrated chaos. Cricket marveled at the innovative and advanced society that lay beneath the ocean's surface.

Cricket's breath caught in her throat as she gazed outside at the breathtaking scenery passing by. The vivid colors blended together, creating a stunning display. But her attention was drawn back to the equally captivating figure of Daimon inside the craft. Every movement he made seemed effortless, like he was one with the vehicle. She could see the muscles in his arms flexing as he worked in perfect tandem with Ashur, navigating them through the changing terrain. It was beyond belief how skilled they were, and Cricket couldn't tear her eyes away from their graceful coordination.

The sisters pressed their faces against the smooth interior of the submarine, eager to catch their first glimpses of the city ahead. Nadine placed her outspread hands on the wall, almost as if she could will it to open up and reveal Atlantis sooner. Cricket noticed how vulnerable and gentle her sister looked in that moment. "We're almost there," Nadine said, her voice carrying over the low hum of the submarine.

The city unfurled like a living tapestry beneath them, intricate patterns of light and shadow playing across structures that defied imagination itself. Cricket's gaze lingered on the ancient pyramids, where the Mer's history was etched in every gleaming facet, their legacy as eternal as the ocean.

The ship glided to a halt at the bustling station, immediately encircled by Mers engaged in their various tasks around the vessel. Cricket's mouth fell open in sheer astonishment. The Mer women adorned themselves in long, flowing gowns of translucent fabric, shimmering with every hue of precious gemstones. These ethereal garments caressed their flawless curves, leaving nothing to the imagination and accentuating their sensuality for all to admire. Their confidence radiated from every movement, creating an aura of effortless allure.

Equally captivating were the Mer men, their chiseled chests exposed and glistening under the ambient light. They wore formfitting skirts that clung to their muscular thighs and ended just above the knee, ensuring that no passerby could overlook their impressive physiques. Their manhood was emphasized with pride, daring observers to avert their eyes. All of them moved gracefully on bare feet, adding an earthy touch to their otherworldly beauty.

Ashur's voice rang out, official and commanding. "Preparing for debark sequence," he announced.

"What's this?" Babs inquired, her eyes widening as Daimon clasped a bronze bracelet adorned with intricate floral patterns around her wrist. The metal glinted softly under the dim light, its craftsmanship delicate yet sturdy. He moved methodically, distributing identical bracelets to each of the sisters. Cricket turned hers over in her hand, marveling at how unexpectedly light it felt, its warmth seeping gently into her skin.

Daimon's lips curled into a knowing smile. "You've just traveled hundreds of feet beneath the ocean's surface," he began, his voice resonating with an air of mystery and playfulness. "These devices will prevent your lungs from collapsing or your blood from boiling"—he paused for dramatic effect, clicking his cheek with a soft pop of his tongue—"among other things."

As the hatch creaked open, Cricket's ears ached under the sudden shift in pressure. A sharp hissing noise reverberated through the cabin, signaling the influx of outside air. Almost immediately, the briny scent of fresh kelp mingled with an unexpectedly earthy aroma wafted in.

As they emerged from the vessel, the sisters' breaths were momentarily stolen by the grandeur towering above them. The massive structures loomed over them, reaching upward with intricate spires and glittering windows. The distant sound of joyful laughter and bustling activity filled the air, creating a sense of lively energy. It was as if the entire city was pulsing with excitement.

"Your aunt and sister should be arriving shortly, Landlings," Daimon reassured them with a gentle smile. "In the meantime, allow me to show you to the guest quarters where you can freshen up and rest after your perilous journey."

The stone floors gleamed beneath their feet as they followed him down a narrow hallway lined with intricate tapestries depicting ancient sea creatures. In this cozy sanctuary, they could take a minute to breathe.

Cricket could barely keep her eyes open, sheer exhaustion weighing down her eyelids like heavy curtains. This new world was a sensory overload, far exceeding her wildest dreams. She had imagined it to be wonderful, but the reality surpassed even her most vivid fantasies with its breathtaking beauty. The air was filled with a soft hum, resonating as though the pyramids themselves were singing their own unique tunes, each contributing to an intricate symphony that reverberated throughout the underwater city. The colors surrounding her were extraordinary — deep purples and blues that seemed to pulse and swirl with a mesmerizing life of their own. As Cricket kept pace with her sisters, she could almost hear the gentle melody of Zadie's voice weaving through this aquatic realm, its soothing tones lulling her into a serene state of tranquility.

CHAPTER 9

ZADIE

Zadie's voice trembled as she reached out, her hand stroking the rough underside of the ship now facing the sky. The unexpected rogue wave had flipped them over completely. Zadie frantically discarded her bulky weather gear and transformed into her Mer form to brave the tumultuous waters. With a surge of power, the tattoo on her skin began to writhe and slither, coming to life. And in an instant, the creature she had always carried with her burst out of her skin and grew to its full two-foot size—a magnificent kraken with shimmering tentacles and glowing eyes.

He swam with fluid grace beside her, his body fully embracing the freedom of the water. His unbridled joy for being immersed in the depths was evident in every stroke, even as the choppy waves threatened to throw him off course. With each undulation of his powerful limbs, he conquered the turbulent sea with ease, a true master of the aquatic world.

Aunt Maj, a regal and commanding presence, adorned in her full suit of Mer armor, gracefully propelled herself through the water toward Zadie. The iridescent scales of her tail shimmered and glinted, catching the flashes of lightning with each powerful stroke. With one swift movement, she reached out and swathed Zadie in a warm embrace, soothing her fears with her comforting presence.

"Your sisters are safe," she assured Zadie as she handed her a small cylindrical bar made of a strange metal. "You remember how to use the keen from when we rescued *Dulcinea*." It was not a question but an expectation. "We will flip the ship back to her upright position." Along with the bar, Maj also gave Zadie a bracelet with a delicate flower design. Zadie quickly fastened it around her wrist and gripped onto the metal bar tightly. She did recognize the tools. She marveled at their advanced technology, intricate design, and flawless craftsmanship.

As Zadie looked around, she saw a sea of at least two dozen of Maj's soldiers emerging from the choppy waves. Their suits of armor gleamed in the lightning, their tools held firmly in hand as they advanced toward Maj. Each soldier had their unwavering gaze fixed on their leader, eager to follow her every command.

Zadie sighed with relief. "I don't know how I would have managed without your answer to my call."

"We will discuss your rash behavior later." Maj's expression remained stoic. "For now, let's concentrate on the task at hand."

Maj lifted her arm, the bracelet reflecting the lightning as she pointed it at *Yara's* capsized form. A chorus of voices joined her, soldiers and Mer alike, their bracelets glowing with ethereal energy that seemed to be pulled from the storm clouds themselves.

With a collective song, the Mer summoned a powerful spell, imbuing the water with dazzling light and pulsing frequency. The waves rose and swelled, lifting the ship out of its submerged state. As if guided by invisible hands, the vessel hovered in the air, suspended by pure magic. The Mer moved beneath it in a graceful dance, their elegant forms weaving intricate patterns as they directed the ship back to the surface. With a final flourish, they lowered it gently back onto the sea, perfectly upright as if it had never faltered. It was a display of pure enchantment, leaving Zadie in awe of the ancient powers wielded by her kin.

The ocean roared and churned as sea water dumped from the windows and deck of the ship. *Yara* undulated, ridding herself of all the extra water. The sails filled with magic, tattered remnants now pulsating with energy as they smoothly repaired themselves, seamlessly weaving together to form one whole sail once again.

Zadie reached out and touched the bottom of *Yara's* rough hull as she swam alongside her. "Are you okay?" Her voice was muffled by the waves.

"My boards are strained. I feel pulled apart." *Yara's* voice echoed in Zadie's mind.

Zadie surveyed her surroundings, watching as every Mer dove beneath the water. They used their keens to propel themselves deeper into the ocean, returning to their home in Atlantis. All except Maj.

Maj spoke with a soft yet resolute tone. "Zadie, she will not survive much longer. You should have never taken such a risk in the Triangle. It was fortunate that we found you and your sisters in time." Maj's flushed cheeks stood out against the angry grey light. Her frustration was evident as her voice rose. "You could have been lost in the tides of time!"

Zadie's cheeks flushed with embarrassment as she took the scolding in silence. How could she have been so stupid? She should have never brought *Yara* to such a dangerous place. But what other choice did she have? This was the only route to Atlantis. If it were just her, she could have swum deep beneath the sea, avoiding the treacherous Triangle altogether. But what about her sisters? They couldn't hold their breath underwater indefinitely. But *Yara* and *Dulcinea* nearly paid a permanent price for her recklessness. A heavy stone formed in her stomach.

Maj placed a finger under Zadie's chin and gently lifted it, urging her to look up. "We'll swim over to her bow and guide her out of the Triangle. Then she can sail safely back to her marina. Is there someone there who can take care of her?"

Tears welled up in Zadie's eyes as she recalled handing Tom all the necessary documentation for *Yara* some time ago. She had bid farewell to Tom, but the realization that she would also have to say goodbye to *Yara* and *Dulcinea* had not fully hit her yet. She sniffed and managed to utter, "Yes, they will be well taken care of."

Zadie's grief mingled with the ocean one salty tear after another. She was able to keep up with Aunt Maj thanks to the use of the keen, the slim stick that propelled them through the turbulent waters and gave her tired tail a break. Kraken clung to her back, his suction cups clinging to her skin tightly. They maneuvered around errant sea vessels and dodged attacks from planes and zeppelins dropping artillery, till finally *Yara* was clear of danger.

The connection between Zadie and *Yara* hummed, a silent conversation flowing through the ether. *Dulcinea's* ethereal presence hovered nearby, an unspoken support during this heartfelt farewell. At least they would have each other.

Zadie's somber voice trembled as she gave her final instructions. "Please return to the marina. Tom will be waiting for you there." Her eyes glistened with unshed tears as she expressed her deep gratitude. "Every moment we've shared together has been a treasure."

Maj eyes went wide. "You mean to stay, permanently?"

Tears shimmered like pearls against Zadie's cheeks. "It's time."

Yara's response, though unheard by the others, resonated within Zadie's mind — a promise to carry out her wishes, a vow of loyalty no matter the distance between them.

Zadie pressed her palm against the hull of the ship one last time, knowing that she would carry the pain of this parting moment forever. "You go with my heart. Both of you."

After a joyous reunion with her sisters, with hours of chattering about their perilous journey and the unbelievable beauty of Atlantis, exhausted and content, Zadie fell into a deep and peaceful slumber, like a precious pearl tucked safely within its shell. She buried her head deeper into the cloudlike bed that cocooned her, wishing to prolong the blissful comfort for just a little while longer. She had never experienced such complete rest before, secure in the depths of the ocean. In this moment, there was nothing that could compare to the sense of peace she felt. It was exactly what she needed after enduring so much loss in such a short time.

But her peaceful slumber was soon disturbed. As morning arrived the room was filled with the lively chatter of her sisters, their voices overlapping and blending together like a symphony.

The rich aroma of freshly brewed coffee filled the air, beckoning her out of bed. After donning a colorful robe, she entered the kitchen to find her siblings gathered around a spread of fresh fruits and steaming bowls of hot cereal. Each bite seemed to fill them with energy. Gwylm drank deeply from a bowl on the ground and ate from a platter of food. Good. They would all need as much strength as they could muster for the journey ahead.

When breakfast was over, they hurriedly dressed in gifted gowns that reflected the oceanic hues, allowing them to fit in with the ladies of this watery realm.

Cricket gracefully twirled in a large circle, admiring the way her blush-colored gown hugged her body. A delicate brooch made of coral adorned one shoulder, adding an elegant touch to the outfit. The fabric cascaded down from her shoulders with a gentle drape, ending in a small train that trailed behind her as she moved. Her satin slippers were secured with matching coral buttons, completing the look perfectly.

The bedroom was adorned with an ornate mirror that spanned one entire wall, reflecting Cricket's image back at her in stunning detail. She continued spinning, admiring her reflection, the delicate folds of her dress, and the intricate beading sparkling under the soft light. "Do you think we get to keep these beautiful dresses?" she asked excitedly, eyes shining with glee.

Babs and Nadine stood side by side, wearing stunning gowns that shimmered deep garnet. Thick strands of pearls wrapped around their necks, gathering the fabric of the dresses at the front right beneath their collarbones, leaving the sides of their breasts and their backs completely exposed. The long, flowing gowns accentuated their athletic builds, with long slits on either side showing off their toned thighs. Satin slippers adorned their feet, adding the finishing touch to their elegant appearance. Nadine's face glowed with delight as she ran her hands down her sides, while

Babs tugged at the fabric of her dress, appearing self-conscious under Zadie's gaze. She straightened her posture and delicately adjusted her crown, which emitted a strange glow that seemed out of place in the room. It was almost as if it were having an adverse reaction to the atmosphere around it.

Zadie's outfit mimicked the styles of Babs and Nadine, but instead of pearls, she wore a chunky bronze collar necklace that held up her flowing azure gown. She adjusted her bronze flower cuff on her wrist and slipped a sharp knife and her keen into a hidden pocket within the folds of her dress. She kept her feet unshod, with the exception of ornamental chains that connected to her toes and coiled around her ankles.

It was as if the ocean floor was calling out to her, begging for her skin to make contact with its surface. Her skin, in turn, was yearning for its touch. She made tiny circles with her toe, caressing the ground. She could feel the deep, ancient power thrumming beneath her feet, coursing through her body with a delicious thrill. It was as though she had been deprived of this energy and was now savoring every pulse of it. How had she ever lived without experiencing this connection?

The warmth of Kraken, in his tattoo form, tingled upon her skin, his tentacles curled around her thigh. The intensity of the storm had taken its toll on him, and she was relieved to know he was finally resting, being recharged.

Nadine hovered by the door. "Everyone ready?"

Zadie looked around as all her sisters nodded in agreement.

The golden streets of Atlantis shimmered beneath Zadie's feet as they passed through an iridescent door, the shimmering divider between their guest quarters and the grand thruway that led to the heart of the city. As they emerged, the splendor of Atlantis unfolded before them. Mers walked with a fluid grace that reflected the sea surrounding them. But amidst all this softness, bronze armor gleamed on the wide chests of the warriors, silently showing their strength and ferocity, both male and female alike.

Zadie contemplated her future and the possibility of joining the warrior class, serving under her aunt. Alternatively, she could live a life as a civil servant. But she didn't feel drawn strongly to either path. She had resisted coming here for so long that she hadn't given much thought to what her life would be like once she arrived.

"It truly is a sight to behold," Babs breathed, her voice reflecting both awe and unease. Gwylm matched her steps as her gaze lingered at the kelp gardens and colorful coral reefs. Marvel reflected in her eyes at how they thrived under the careful touch of the caretakers that wove in and out of the beds. All wore flowing green gowns that gathered just below their breasts.

Nadine nodded, her eyes taking in the mesmerizing sight of this sunken city. "Its beauty is unmatched," she murmured, "even in comparison to the majestic ice palaces of the winter court." Her normally flawless skin seemed almost translucent against the vibrant backdrop.

Cricket's gaze skittered up the vast spires and across the immense pyramids. "My wings long to soar, I wish to see it all up close. This place is like a dream."

Zadie's own heart danced a complex rhythm.

"Welcome to Atlantis." Daimon's voice sliced through her thoughts, his presence commanding attention despite his casual saunter. He and Aunt Maj were closing the distance between the two parties. His eyes locked with Zadie's, and a wave of familiarity washed over her. A warmth started at the pit of her stomach and extended, pulsating throughout. Her vision narrowed as tiny pricks of starlight seemed to surround them. "Ready for a journey of fates?" he asked.

"I'm sorry," Zadie stuttered. "Have we met before?" He felt so familiar.

Daimon gave a smoldering grin. "You recognize my magic, for it is what your magic draws from." He waved his hand across the vast city. "For we are all one. One magic." He glanced at Babs's crown. "Unlike our land-dwelling cousins, our power comes not from relics."

Was Zadie imagining or was there a playful challenge within his words?

Babs opened her mouth to object.

Aunt Maj lifted a hand and shook her finger at Babs before voicing, "Banter later. Daimon, I wish to send my nieces home as soon as possible." Her tone made it clear that her decision was final and there would be no room for argument.

Daimon raised an eyebrow, clearly shocked at being spoken to in such a manner.

"Lead the way to the temple," she commanded, obviously ignoring his questioning manner. "Ashur and I have spoken. We are in agreement."

Daimon shrugged and turned, his gait light and unbothered as he followed her bidding.

They followed closely behind, matching his steps. Zadie examined her aunt. Today, she had ditched her usual armor and instead was wearing a sheer dress that hung lightly on one shoulder, leaving the other one bare. The skirt of the dress flowed behind her as she walked, her bare feet gliding lightly against the cool path. With her hair styled in loose waves piled high on top of her head, she had a soft and delicate appearance that was contrary to how Zadie thought of her.

Zadie trailed just a breath behind Daimon. She admired his broad, muscular shoulders. His bare chest was adorned with a large garnet set in bronze, proudly displayed at the center. It was larger than her fist. The lines of his shendyt, made of shimmering fabric, were close-fitting. It accentuated the curve of his well-toned bottom and ended just above his knees. She could see how this traditional clothing style, reminiscent of ancient times, would make it easy for him to transform from his human form to Mer.

He raised his arm with a flourish. "The Temple of Destiny," he announced. Looming ahead, an imposing pyramid stood sentinel at the center of the city. Its walls were etched with ancient art, tales of gods and long forgotten monsters intertwined in stone.

"Within these walls lie the secrets of the timelines," Daimon said, his hand gesturing toward the grand entrance again, where colossal doors awaited them. "I'm sure you have heard the legends surrounding the Tablets of Destiny. Ashur is the keeper of the tablets, therefore the temple."

"That isn't right." Babs's eyes drilled into Daimon, her footsteps halting. "Why would the 'keeper of the tablets' risk his life to save us from a shipwreck?" Gwylm seemingly sensed the shift in Babs's mood, and his body language changed accordingly. He hunched his shoulders, his fur standing on end, and let out a low growl.

Nadine, picking up on Babs's alarm, raised her arms as if readying for a fight. "For that matter, who are you in this place?"

Maj exhaled in exasperation. "Girls!"

Daimon smiled, his posture loose and inviting, as if he had all the time in the world to stand on the threshold and enjoy small talk. "First off, the time storms could never harm a Son of Tiamat. Fortunately for Ashur and me, that is precisely who we are. Second, we are the only two that could grant you passage to Atlantis. Only Mer are allowed. This one allowance was at the insistence of Maj." His lips formed a wicked smile. "What exactly have you done to my brother to have him bend to your will? You will have to teach me your secrets."

Maj rolled her eyes and smiled, glancing down at her perfectly proportioned figure. "It's a secret power that you are not capable of wielding—over him, at least."

Daimon chuckled heartily, his laugh free of any concern. "I understand now," he said, shaking his head with mock exaggeration. "May Tiamat protect me from such a destiny." He shifted his gaze back to the temple doors and pushed them open wide.

Zadie felt a strong pull toward what lay ahead of her. She caught the unmistakable aroma of burning incense, with hints of sandalwood, lavender, and myrrh wafting through her nostrils. It brought to mind ancient ceremonies and rituals, triggering a sense of nostalgia and forgotten recollections within her. It was as if the secrets and enigmas were just out of reach.

Nadine whispered to herself, her eyes alight with wonder.

Aunt Maj's eyes scanned over her nieces, as if they were little kittens that needed to be gathered and tended to.

Zadie cast a final glance at the golden streets, and the Mer who walked upon them oblivious to the crossroads at which she now stood. With a steadying breath, she crossed the threshold of the temple, the shadows of ancient knowledge surrounding her as the doors closed behind, as they ventured deeper into the very heart of Atlantis.

The silence of the Temple of Destiny was a living thing, pulsing with the heartbeat of unseen magic. The intense humidity caused condensation to trickle down the steep slopes of the glass peak of the pyramid that audibly sizzled when it found its way to the thick stone walls, filling the interior atmosphere with a strange thick mist. Zadie's eyes widened as she stepped further into the sanctum, her gaze drawn to the peculiar sight of hybrid creatures meandering amongst the dense foliage that seemed to grow without constraint.

Chained at their necks, the beings moved with an otherworldly elegance in the filtered light streaming through the high windows. Their forms were both alluring and grotesque, with humanlike heads featuring large almond-shaped eyes that were a deep black, devoid of emotion. However, their bodies were a mixture of different creatures—some had low-slung bodies with scaly hides resembling alligators, while others had large, padded feet like lions. The procession was led by priestesses wearing revealing attire leaving little to the imagination as they guided the hybrids along. The creatures seemed to move in a trancelike state, as if under the influence of a powerful spell cast by the maidens.

"Careful," Daimon murmured, close enough for his breath to brush against Zadie's ear. "Their chains are not just for show."

Zadie nodded, her focus never leaving the ethereal dance before her. The tropical plants surrounding them released a fragrance that was intoxicating, mingling with incense to cloud her thoughts with a sense of euphoria.

"Are they prisoners?" Nadine asked, her voice laced with anger.

"Prisoners of time, perhaps," Aunt Maj replied, cryptic as ever.

Cricket clutched at Zadie's arm as Babs remained silent, her expression unreadable, but her protective stance beside Cricket spoke volumes.

As they ventured deeper, Zadie's attention was snared by the temple maidens who tended to the magical pools scattered throughout the chamber. The waters shimmered with an inner light, casting reflections upon the maidens' focused faces. They moved with purpose, their hands occasionally dipping into the liquid, emerging with what looked like strands of pure luminescence thickly seeping between their fingers.

Above the pools, scrolls and books were nestled within covered alcoves deeply carved into the walls, each tome radiating an aura of significance. Zadie's heart thrummed with the realization of the knowledge housed within these sacred confines—the annals of destinies shaped and reshaped, the compendiums of time itself.

"Such power," Zadie murmured, half to herself, feeling the pull of an ancient instinct to delve into the secrets held within those pages.

Taking in her gaze, Daimon asked, "Are you called to be priestess?" A smile flirted at the corners of his reddened lips. "Maj said you were staying. I'm happy to hear it."

"Her place will not be decided today," Maj declared, grabbing Zadie by the elbow.

Zadie cast a final glance at the enigmatic scenery around her. This was a place of boundless knowledge and unfathomable control. Not where the threads of fate were spun, weaved, and cut, but where they were judged worthy or unworthy. If deemed unworthy, that future would be sealed off and banished from the world above. But who exactly made these decisions?

Gran had given the crown to Maj to hide here. She fully believed it could not be obtained ever again. According to Cricket, her last words to Sabella said as much. Zadie's stomach turned upside down, and she feared she might vomit. This felt wrong.

"Ashur," Daimon greeted the proud and regal figure that approached them. He was dressed much like his brother, with the minor difference that the stone that graced his chest was a huge stone of lapis lazuli, set not in bronze but in thick green jade covered in mysterious symbols.

"Brother." Ashur inclined his head slightly, then turned his attention to Maj. "You speak on behalf of your kin?"

Maj inclined her head deeply. "It is as you say." She kept her eyes averted, as if waiting.

Ashur scanned the sisters, his serious eyes landing on Zadie. She felt stripped naked under his intense gaze as if he knew her every thought. Her unease rose with every moment that passed. "Your task is not a welcomed one," he intoned with a voice that seemed to harmonize with the currents themselves. "Why should we allow such a reckless act? It is not wise to open a sealed path."

The words washed over her, causing a wave of uncertainty, and for a moment, Zadie felt the pull of his reasoning tugging at her mind. She knew he spoke the truth. The path should not be opened.

"But"—Daimon laid his hand upon the garnet at the center of his chest—"opening a path is not unheard of." He glanced at Maj, his lips hinting at a smile as he quickly winked at her. Maj pursed her lips and narrowed her eyes.

Babs, unable to contain herself any longer, blurted, "We will leave with the winter crown." Her fangs were visible between her parted red lips. "Or die trying."

Cricket laid a light hand on Babs's shoulder.

Ashur's eyes widened. "Lieutenant General, your kin show a lack of manners."

Maj opened her mouth to respond.

With a dramatic gesture, Nadine put her back to Babs, and sparks flew between the twins as Nadine released a powerful blast of fire from her hands. The force of the flames caused a whirlwind to swirl around them both.

The outburst reverberated through the hollow chambers, a harsh contrast to the serene faces of the temple maidens who continued their work as if such displays were mundane and of no concern. In the silence that followed, Zadie's heart wrestled with conflicting loyalties. She knew they needed to retrieve the crown and deliver it to the winter king so that he would free their father to return to a simple human life with their mother. But deep in her gut, she felt Ashur was speaking the truth. This was dangerous and would create unseen consequences. Was it truly worth that risk?

Ashur furrowed his brow and addressed Maj. "The young ones of your line are little more than wild beasts. I have a mind to send them on their way." His face contorted into a frown, like he had just tasted something unpleasant.

"Brother," Daimon chided. "Have patience with them. Their reason is sound. The request is from a place of love. What wouldn't you and I have done if we could have saved our—"

Ashur burst out, "Speak no more, Daimon!"

Zadie recoiled at Ashur's harsh words, spoken with such rage, or was it pain? But how could that be if he wielded such power? Her skin crawled as a hush fell upon her heart, the distant melody of the temple's enchantments ringing in her ears. Could it be that this place of beauty and knowledge was also a cage for those bound to its service? Even ones as powerful as Ashur and Daimon? If that was the price for them, she wondered, briefly, what the price would be for her.

Maj's voice broke the quiet, her eyes searching, pleading with an intensity that startled Zadie. "Ash, please, for me—" she whispered.

Daimon grinned widely, a sparkle in his eye, as if he had understood what had been said between the lines. "Oh, Ash, do—do it for her," he teased.

The room held its breath, waiting for Ashur to speak, to deny or accept their request. One word would determine the future of the Culebra line. Their fate rested in his hands.

Ashur's hand swept across the room, drawing attention to the frescoes that adorned the walls of the temple—scenes of Mer warriors in battle, their tails like silvered daggers slicing through waves. "Our history is as deep and fathomless as the ocean itself," he began, his voice a deep undercurrent that pulled Zadie into the ripples of the past.

"Once, we ruled the surface," Daimon added, his presence as commanding as the tides. "Our mother, Tiamat, the queen of all waters. But betrayal came like a tempest, and she was overthrown, forced to retreat to these submerged sanctuaries. And we—" His voice trailed as he touched the stone that lay on his chest.

"Each realm of existence, every timeline that ever was or will be, flows from the heart of Atlantis, the Temple of Destiny," Ashur continued, his gaze grazing over the sisters, then locking with Zadie's. "We Mer are its custodians, bound to its ebb and flow, preservers of the continuum."

Zadie absorbed their words, the weight of eons and the burden of infinity teasing at her mind like a mantle of sea-weed. She could see it in their eyes — the solemn duty that anchored them to this underwater realm, as unyielding and ragged as coral.

Nadine stepped forward, her silver eyes ablaze with a fervor that cut through the somber tones of the chamber. "We need to find the crown," she demanded, her voice crackling with the fire of her lineage. "Our father languishes in the winter court's dungeons because of its absence. Help us retrieve it, and I can finally lead him back to the warmth of home, to Mama's waiting arms."

"Your yearning for a life taken from you resonates within me," Daimon acknowledged, as if he knew her deepest secrets, her darkest moments of despair. "The desire to reunite your family is noble."

Ashur studied Nadine, the lines of his face etched with the wisdom of ages. With a gentle touch, he connected with the ancient stone resting on his chest. His eyes glowed with mystic power as he communed with the gem. And just like a statue come to life, he stood tall and unwavering, ready to wield the magic within him. "To set the timelines aright, the crown must indeed be returned. It is needed to balance the realms above. Our time of being its custodian is indeed to be at an end. Our resources are at your disposal."

Ashur's proclamation reverberated through the temple, each word a pebble plunging into the depths of Zadie's conscience. "The timeline will be opened for you," he declared, his voice an amalgam of thunderous power and a whispering tide. "But heed this — once the current of time is disturbed, it can ensnare as easily as it flows. Should you become trapped in a failed timeline, your existence will ebb into nothingness, lost to all but memory."

Zadie's breath caught, the grim reality of Ashur's warning coiling around her like a cold sea serpent. The stakes were monumental, yet the call to rescue their father and restore balance demanded they dare the treacherous waters of fate.

Aunt Maj stepped forward, her hand resting lightly on Ashur's forearm. Her face was alight with confidence, her voice light and resolute. "I will aid in keeping the portal stable," she proclaimed, her tone unequivocal, a lighthouse guiding them through the impending storm. "My powers shall serve as an anchor amidst the tempest of disruption."

"Thank you, Aunt Maj," Nadine breathed, her gratitude written on her face.

Babs clenched her fists, the muscles in her jaw tightening, while Cricket's eyes darted between the sisters and their formidable aunt, the gravity of their undertaking mirrored in her wide gaze.

Zadie remained silent, her thoughts churning. The knowledge that one misstep could unmoor them from existence itself was daunting. With Aunt Maj's support, the path forward seemed less insurmountable, the darkness ahead pierced by the faintest glimmer of hope.

Daimon's silhouette cut through the ambient glow of bioluminescent algae that adorned the temple walls. A smirk played at the corners of his mouth, but his eyes betrayed a gravity Zadie had not witnessed before. "I shall accompany you," he declared, his voice threading through the heavy air like an anchor line into the depths.

The sisters paused, their attention drawn to him in unison. Zadie felt a flutter within, a mingling of uncertainty and unexpected warmth. Whether it was the trepidation of the journey or the inexplicable comfort Daimon's presence brought, she couldn't decide.

"Your knowledge of the timelines will prove invaluable," Ashur intoned from beside the magical pools, nodding in approval.

"Thank you, Daimon," Zadie said, her voice steady despite the whirlpool of emotions within her. She turned then to Ashur, the regal bearing of the elder Mer resonating with the ancient power of Atlantis itself. "And to you, Ashur, for granting us passage."

Ashur merely inclined his head.

Lastly, Zadie's gaze found Aunt Maj, her warrior's stance unwavering. "Without your strength to anchor the portal, we would be adrift. Without you—"

Aunt Maj's lips parted in what might have been the beginning of a smile. "Family binds tighter than the strongest currents, Zadie. Go with the tides of my blessing and come back to me. Take your place by my side."

Zadie's fingers traced the intricate carvings of the temple walls, her touch lingering on the warm stone as if to draw courage from its ancient wisdom.

Babs, Cricket, and Nadine appeared calm on the surface, but there was an underlying tension in their demeanor that revealed their true feelings of anxiety.

Maj handed Babs a satchel filled to the brim. "Everything I could think of that may be of help."

Babs's shoulders dropped, and a smile crossed her face. "Thank you."

"Then it's time." There was a finality in Maj's words.

Zadie looked at her sisters, seeing the reflection of her own trepidation mirrored in their eyes. She took a deep breath, letting the heady thick air fill her lungs, steadying her spirit.

With a nod to Daimon, who returned the gesture with a knowing look, they moved toward an indentation in the wall of the temple about five inches deep in the shape of a door. Aunt Maj touched one open palm to the outline of the indentation and stared into Ashur's eyes. "I'm ready."

Ashur stretched his arms toward the towering pyramid, giving himself over to its ancient magic. His body began to tremble and contort in unnatural ways as he channeled the magic within. A bright blue light emanated from his skin, blinding those who dared to look directly at him. His muscles rippled and expanded with newfound strength, causing his skin to stretch and change color. Bright green, blue, and silver scales sprouted from his body, giving him a shimmering and majestic appearance.

A brilliant light emanated from the stone at his breast, glowing with a power that seemed to come from outside of time. As he completed his transformation into a mighty dragon, the air was filled with the whoosh of his unfurling wings, their impressive span filling the space around him. Zadie's gaze traveled over his massive form, noticing intricate designs etched into each scale. The ancient writings glowed with an eerie green light, pulsing in sync with the rhythm of his breath rippling from the stone at his heart. It was as if he were a living canvas, adorned with markings that held secrets that Zadie could not even guess at.

The massive dragon lowered his head, getting closer to Maj. With her arm outstretched, she managed to bridge the gap between the dragon and the cutout in the wall. A mysterious aura emanated from the cutout's center. The deep blue hue shimmered and swirled, revealing glimpses of distant galaxies and sparkling constellations. Zadie couldn't resist stepping closer as the magic of the swirling stars beckoned.

Daimon positioned himself in front of Zadie and motioned for her sisters to follow. Without hesitation, Nadine flew past them with Babs and Gwylm close behind. Cricket shrugged sheepishly at Zadie before falling into step be-hind Babs.

As Daimon's shoulder brushed against Zadie, a warm sensation spread throughout her body. It was an unexpected feeling of comfort that eased her uncertainty. Once again, she felt a sense of familiarity and allowed herself to f e e l happy, if only for a moment.

"It looks like we'll bring up the rear," Daimon whispered. "Stay close."

Zadie gave him a small but genuine smile. "If you insist."

CHAPTER 10

NADINE

Nadine's feet sank into the scorching sand, her breath hitched in shock as she emerged first from the swirling portal. The desert welcomed them with a suffocating stillness, devoid of any signs of life. Shifting figures lurked between the bare trees. It was more like she could sense them than see them. The unrelenting heat clawed at her skin. It was like being trapped in an all-encompassing oven, with no escape from the sweltering torment.

Babs materialized from the vortex's glow, a vigilant sentinel with eyes that missed nothing. Her long hair appeared almost iridescent in the evening light, and her lithe form moved with a predator's grace. Gwylm, ever at her side, was poised for any threat that might spring from the arid desert. Nadine couldn't be more proud of the woman her sister had become. It was a long time coming. Babs had been a whiney baby for most of her life. Nadine did her best to toughen her up. Yet, since she had finished the challenges and donned the crown, Babs had a hard edge to her. Nadine respected that.

The once vibrant and lively wings of Cricket now hung limply as she fought against the unyielding desert winds. To Nadine, she resembled a dying flower in a vase that had been left for too long. The scorching heat beat down on her delicate frame, her paper-thin wings offering little defense. Cricket grumbled to herself, scolding her lack of foresight for venturing into this unknown terrain without considering the weather conditions.

Nadine rolled her eyes. The very idea that Cricket ever thought one step ahead, let alone two, was laughable. Nadine had spent years observing from the sidelines as her sister ricocheted from one situation to another like a pinball in a chaotic game. Cricket's life was a series of knee-jerk reactions rather than deliberate actions. Pathetic. Yet, despite her exasperation, Nadine struggled to muster some sympathy for Cricket. After all, she had just endured the harrowing ordeal of witnessing Gran's brutal death. But quitting at the first sign of trouble? How could anyone be so defeatist? She wouldn't last a day in the winter court. Among her three sisters, Cricket remained the most enigmatic and hardest for Nadine to comprehend.

The unforgiving heat began to leave red patches on Daimon's bare chest and back. His shendyt fluttered in the hot wind, not shielding him in the least. Despite his obvious discomfort, he stood resolute, his gaze sweeping over the scorching terrain. As grains of sand clung to his slick skin, they formed wet streaks down his strong frame, glistening like droplets of sweat. Nadine wondered if he and Zadie would cope being so far from the ocean they both called home.

Nadine shielded her eyes from the blowing sand of this unfamiliar land. As her vision adjusted, she noticed the striking resemblance between Daimon and Ambrosias, the winter prince. She had grown up in the shadow of the prince; she knew him well. The sharp angles of his jawline and watchful blue eyes were nearly identical to those of Ambrosias. It was uncanny, as if they shared a long-forgotten lineage. Nadine's mind raced with wild theories — could there be a connection between the bloodlines of the courts and the mysterious Mer living beneath the sea? She shook her head in disbelief.

Close behind him, Zadie's bare feet imprinted a delicate and fleeting trail in the desert floor. Each step left a subtle mark on the fine, powdery sand, like whispers of her presence that would soon be erased by the shifting winds. The heat radiated from the ground, creating mirages that danced in her wake. If it was this hot at night, how would they survive the day? They would just have to work fast. Real fast.

Babs was the first to speak. "So, I guess water-dragon isn't just a title."

Nadine brushed a stray hair out of her face, putting her hands on her hips and leaning to one side. "Are you and your brother, Ashur, alike? Do you both have the ability to transform?"

Daimon smiled a wide grin, reminding Nadine of a puppy dog. "Ashur and I are as different in temperament and abilities as could be. I'm guessing the four of you can understand that."

Babs rolled her eyes. "Oh yeah, we get that. Even as sisters, we are all very different."

Cricket interrupted, emphasizing her point with a gentle wave of her hand. "But at the core, we are still similar, Babs." She brushed her hair out of her eyes. "I'm sure as water-dragons with the same magical abilities, you must be more alike than not?"

Daimon shifted his weight from one side to the other. Nadine could see beads of perspiration forming on his skin. "Ashur is responsible for the Tablet of Destiny and overseeing the temple. He doesn't guess the future, he directs it. In a way, he is it."

Zadie used her toe to draw a small circle in the sand, avoiding eye contact as she asked, "And what about you? What are you responsible for?" She bit her lower lip and looked up through her lashes.

Daimon let out a loud barking laugh. His merriment sparkled through his eyes. "Anything my big brother tells me to do—such as escorting you into a failed timeline to retrieve a crown." He laughed again. "Yep, this is exactly the kind of thing that becomes my responsibility."

Nadine's gaze swept over her sisters' scantily clad bodies, their skin already flushing a tender pink under the relentless heat. Zadie's bare feet were gradually turning crimson from the searing warmth radiating off the ground. If nothing was done soon, painful blisters and bleeding would be inevitable. *Idiot*, Nadine thought bitterly. *Who embarks on a journey barefoot?* They all scanned their surroundings. The sky was filled with shades of purple and blue, while flickers of what appeared to be fireflies danced through bare tree limbs—an oddly enchanting sight. Nadine was perplexed by her inability to locate where the ambient light was coming from in the darkened sky.

Cricket scanned the horizon. "Well, Daimon. This is turning out to be quite the big responsibility. How are we going to find water? Shelter? This is quite a quest we are on."

Even in this stifling and harsh environment, Daimon's body emanated coolness and strength. His muscles shifted and flexed, almost like water rippling through his body instead of muscle and bone. His black hair stood out against the white sand, and his focused blue eyes glinted in the waning light. "We will work together," he proclaimed.

Nadine's throat felt like it was on fire as she swallowed, each passing moment of this stifling heat draining her energy. She was used to the icy grip of the winter court, where she thrived in its frigid embrace. But now, surrounded by her weak and feeble sisters, she reached deep within herself to find strength. Perhaps if she could help them, their opinions of her would soften. She had to admit, she hadn't given them much reason to like her. It was against her very nature to rely on anyone else, she was so used to being on her own. But maybe, just maybe, things could be different — she could be different. Maybe, things could be — better. Her voice was subdued. "Spread out."

With practiced and precise movements, Nadine raised her palms skyward, the graceful dance of her fingers weaving an ancient pattern in the air. The fire magic of her ancestors responded to her call, intensifying the heat around them. But just as quickly, nature answered with a cascading downpour from the heavens above. The once stifling air was now charged with the refreshing scent of rain. Dark clouds gathered and released their cooling waters onto the parched land below. Zadie's face visibly relaxed in relief, while Cricket eagerly opened her mouth to drink in the nourishing water. Both reveled in the much-needed respite.

"Better?" Nadine asked, her lips curving upward in a rare smile as she maintained the spell with a steady focus.

"Much," Babs replied, her own powers subtly augmenting the coolness with a hint of summer's caress.

"Thank you, Nadine," Zadie said, her tone earnest.

Point for me, Nadine thought.

Daimon frowned. "So much for going undetected." He crossed his arms. "Don't waste your energy on a continuous spell. He reached for the bracelet on his wrist. The bronze metal gleamed in the fading light, adorned with a delicate floral design. He twisted the center button of the bracelet, causing a faint blue glow to emanate from it. The light grew brighter and wrapped around his body. Blue pulsated, engulfing him fully, making him stand out as an indigo stain against the barren landscape.

He gestured toward the bracelet on Zadie's wrist. She mimicked Daimon's motions, her fingers tracing the engraved patterns, and watched in awe as the azure aura bubbled up around her like a second skin. "It's cool! I'm practically chilled!"

Babs's face twisted into an incredulous expression, her lips puckering together in disbelief. "What sorcery is this?" she exclaimed.

Daimon let out a hearty laugh, sounding completely amused. "There's no magic here, Summer Princess. Just technology. It collects moisture from the air and circulates it through your body. See for yourself." Daimon gestured toward Nadine's and Babs's wrists. The devices had been strapped on since their arrival.

With a flick of their wrists, they each activated the delicate bracelets. Nadine's hand trembled slightly as she released her control over the fiery spell that had been swirling around her fingertips.

Each footfall was a measured crunch on the dry desert floor, echoing through the stillness of the night. They pressed on, venturing further into the desolate landscape where the symphony of nocturnal creatures filled the air. The darkness seemed to have engulfed the land.

"Keep your senses open," Babs said, casting a protective glance toward her sisters, ready to erupt should danger present itself. "We are not alone; of that much I am certain."

Impatience simmered within Nadine as she watched Daimon guide them deeper into the unknown. Her gut twisted with unease, and every hair on her neck prickled in alarm. The air felt thick with unseen threats, yet her eyes detected only shadows. "Daimon," she called out, her voice tinged with frustration as she addressed him. "We're here. Now what? How do we find the crown?" She was uncertain about their next move and despised having to seek his guidance.

His laughter was a low rumble. "The magic of the courts does not elude my senses." And with a flourish, Daimon stepped forward, touching the red stone at his breast, his form blurring, twisting, reshaping into something grand and formidable.

There, before them, he became a behemoth of copper-tinged scales and serpentine grace—a water-dragon of such magnificence that the very air around them thrummed with power. His sapphire eyes held the depth of the ocean's secrets, and when he spoke, his voice boomed like the tides. "In this form, I am attuned to the whispers of magic that course through this realm of in-between. Follow me, and the crown will reveal itself."

"Show off much?" Nadine quipped. If he meant to impress, well, it would take more than size. She gave him a second glance. Maybe.

"Through shadows and sand, we shall carve our passage. We find ourselves between the two rivers," Daimon declared, his colossal frame setting into motion, his tail leaving a cleared trail for them to follow.

Cricket dragged her feet, grumbling, "All I can see is the vast expanse of the night sky, starless as it is." She swatted at a mosquito on her arm. "And feel the pesky bugs." She turned to look at Daimon incredulously. "Do you actually see two rivers?"

His scales displayed a beautiful array of autumn hues — rich reds and bright oranges that glimmered in the evening light. He chuckled. "I can smell the water." Then he turned to Zadie, asking, "Can you smell it too?"

Zadie nodded as a smile crossed her face.

The group traversed the desert, their steps muffled. Daimon's golden scales had vanished from sight, thanks to Babs's swift intervention; her hands had weaved through the air with the grace of a seasoned maestro, casting an intricate glamor that rendered the massive dragon unseen to any prying eyes.

Babs explained, "Invisibility should spare us unwanted encounters."

Nadine berated herself for summoning the rain. She hadn't considered that her action would alert everyone to their presence. The hairs on the back of her neck stood on end — a primal alert to the danger that lurked just beyond perception.

"Everything okay back there?" Daimon's tone was devoid of its usual levity.

Each sister mumbled in the affirmative.

Daimon continued, "Tiamat, my mother, birthed eleven abominations, concealed across the frayed edges of time. They are cunning, ruthless — each one a sentinel of peril locked away in these forsaken lands, on the outskirts of time."

Nadine exchanged a glance with her sisters; there was no mistaking the severity in his warning. The very air felt charged, as if the desert itself held its breath, waiting for the creatures of Tiamat's making to emerge from their hidden lairs.

"Your mom is the mother of monsters? You guys must have had quite the family get-togethers." Zadie's hushed words escaped her lips.

She reached down into the concealed pockets of her dress and produced a shining knife, its sharp edge glinting in the dim light. She took on a defensive posture, prepared to fight.

"I thought our family was messy," Nadine said, steeling herself for whatever awaited them in the darkness.

The shadows flickered among the bushes, playing a game of hide-and-seek. Nadine couldn't shake off the feeling of being watched, as if someone was studying their every move from the darkness. Her gaze darted from shadow to shadow, searching for any sign of the lurking dangers Daimon had warned them about. She mulled over what he had disclosed. If Tiamat was the mother of monsters, what did that make him?

Hours passed, marked only by the shifting of sand beneath their feet and the eerie noises that sometimes pierced the stillness—a distant howl or the creak of ancient brush bending under the weight of time. The world seemed to shrink around them.

"The crown is near." Daimon's voice was a resonant thrum that vibrated through the humid air. His invisible form loomed in front of them. "I can feel the chill of winter's magic—it's stronger here."

The darkened grove seemed to whisper a warning, but they pressed on, drawn toward the looming ziggurat in the center. As they approached, flickering lights from within cast haunting shadows on the surrounding trees.

Cricket whispered, "It looks like we've found the local hang out."

Nadine's heart raced as they entered the clearing, greeted by a multitude of statues frozen in fear or shock. Their forms were so lifelike that Nadine's breath hitched in her throat. Each figure was caught in a moment of terror or surprise, their expressions etched in stone forevermore.

"Be wary," Daimon cautioned, his tone laced with an edge. "These were once living creatures, ensnared by a power that does not forgive trespassers."

Nadine reached out, her fingertips skimming along the warm cheek of a statue—a young boy, his eyes wide with unspoken pleas. "What could this mean?" she breathed.

The group exchanged glances, each face mirroring the other's trepidation. Silence fell over the grove of statues, their stone gazes locked eternally on the intruders trespassing in this sacred space. Babs, her movements hurried and determined, moved closer to Daimon. "Tell me of Tiamat," she urged, her voice a low plea. "Tell me of your mother."

Daimon's eyes gleamed with an ancient light as he spoke, words laced with reverence and warning. "My mother is the maelstrom of creation, the whirlwind of chaos and destruction from which all worlds are born." His gaze swept over the frozen tableau around them. "She is both the artist and the art; the life giver and the life taker."

The air changed then, thickening with dread, as if the very mention of Tiamat's name had summoned forth a darkness eager to prove his point.

Out of the inky shadows, a creature emerged. Its massive frame was a terrifying fusion of dragon and lion, with sharp horns jutting out from its head and claws like daggers glinting in the moonlight. It let out a deafening roar that shook the very earth beneath it, and its beady, glowing eyes seemed to penetrate through the darkness and into one's soul. This was not just any ordinary beast; it was an embodiment of pure terror and fear. A low growl emanated from its throat.

As Babs dropped her invisibility spell, Nadine's eyes were dazzled by the sight of Daimon's colossal dragon form that stood directly beside her.

Daimon's warning echoed through the grove. "Don't look Sumgal in the eyes, lest you be turned to stone."

Sumgal shook his mane. "You are far from your home, water-dragon. Tonight I will drag your traitorous corpse before all and don the heart of the worlds on my own breast."

Daimon touched the garnet that dominated his chest. "Sumgal, you are unworthy of such power."

Sumgal moved in a calculated arc, asserting his dominance as he spoke. "I embody courage, strength, resilience, and power." He studied each of them, searching for any weaknesses or vulnerabilities.

"Behind me!" Nadine's command cut through the banter. They sprang into action, their movements a dance of will. Gwylm pushed past Nadine and snarled at the beast.

Sumgal launched forward, his massive dragon jaws snapping with razor-sharp teeth and its lion-like claws swiping through the air with deadly accuracy. The sound of its powerful wings flapping filled the air as it soared toward its target, ready to strike with lethal force. Its scaly body glinted, reflecting a rainbow of colors as it moved.

Nadine swallowed her fear and channeled her fire magic. Her hands moved in fluid, intricate patterns that conjured flames to surround and engulf the monstrous creature in front of her. "Gwylm, move back!" she cried. The searing heat radiated off the flames, causing sweat to drip down Nadine's forehead. She narrowed her gaze, focusing on a spot just above Sumgal's writhing form, willing the fire to consume him completely. A deafening screech pierced the air, making her ears ring, but Nadine refused to back down.

Babs, ever the quick thinker, called upon the elements, and the skies responded with a tempestuous fury. Bolts of lightning crashed down, each strike a targeted assault upon the writhing hybrid.

Cricket, her airy wings unfurled, rose above the fray, the very embodiment of grace under pressure. In contrast, Sumgal's lion-like form seethed with fury as he raised his massive head to face his tiny adversary. The beast lunged upward, its roars shaking the very ground they stood on. Breathless, Cricket deliberately drew the monster's attention toward her, creating an opening for a potential attack from below.

Nadine could see the heat of Sumgal's breath on Cricket's skin. Every muscle in Nadine's body tensed as she prepared for the inevitable battle ahead. This was no ordinary creature—it was a force of nature, fueled by rage and hunger. But she would not cower in his presence; she would stand her ground, and her sisters would witness her bravery.

Daimon, his body swelling and reshaping, grew larger as the glorious form of the golden water-dragon, his colors ever changing, and morphed to the task of taking on Tiamat's abomination. They met head-on, scales clashing against scales in a brutal display of violence. Their guttural roars echoed through the grove, a deafening cacophony of primal sound that induced fear in all.

Statues crumbled under the force of their struggle, once silent witnesses now reduced to rubble. Blood stained the pristine sand. Dry brush caught in the crossfire blazed with an infernal light, casting flickering shadows that danced macabrely across the carnage.

Nadine pushed the heat within her higher, the flames intensifying until they became an inferno that consumed fur and scale. The creature's immense form writhed and twisted, pushing against the onslaught of flames. Once gleaming scales were now blackened and charred, evidence of his valiant struggle to survive. Powerful muscles strained and flexed under his scaly exterior, every movement calculated and determined. And yet he continued to fight on, refusing to yield to the flames that threatened to consume.

Babs shouted incoherent incantations. The raw power of nature surged through her, lending strength to the assault as they cornered the horror of nature before them.

Their unity was their strength, each playing their part in the symphony of survival.

Zadie's voice, usually as melodious and gentle as the sea, now rose in a crescendo of urgency. The words of an ancient sleeping spell wove through the tumultuous air, seeking to impose slumber upon the chaotic maelstrom before her. But the creature of Tiamat was beyond such meager enchantments; it raged on, indifferent to the lyrical plea for peace.

"Sleep," she implored, the magic flickering like a lighthouse beset by stormy waves. It was not to be—the beast roiled, his mass and fury unchecked. With a violent heave, he lunged forward and pinned Zadie to the ground. As if in slow motion, he rolled his massive body upon her. A sickening crunch reverberated through the grove as Zadie was crushed beneath the titan.

"Zadie!" Nadine cried out, her heart sinking as dread knotted in her stomach.

Nadine stood frozen, her heart racing as she watched Zadie's lifeless body revealed as the monster rolled off her. Zadie's limbs were twisted in unnatural positions, bent at odd angles as she lay crumpled on the desert ground. Her body was lifeless, like a rag doll, soaked in a pool of blood that continued to grow. The monstrous creature left his raking mark. Sharp claws dripped with Zadie's blood as Sumgal stared hungrily at his latest victim.

Nadine trembled at the sight, unable to tear her eyes away from the gruesome scene before her.

Babs skidded to her sister's side, her fangs flashing in the firelight as she bit down on her own wrist. The blood that flowed was imbued with life itself, a gift of the summer court—a healing elixir potent enough to mend the gravest of injuries.

"Drink, sister," Babs commanded, pressing her bleeding arm to Zadie's lips. "You will not leave us." Gwylm rushed to Zadie's fallen form.

Zadie's once vibrant skin had taken on a sickly grey hue, making her appear almost ghostlike. Her lips were now a deep shade of purple, a sharp contrast to the paleness of her face. As Babs pleaded urgently for a response, she could only stare in horror at Zadie's rolled-back eyes, showing nothing but white. It was as if all life had been wrenched from her body by those monstrous paws.

Babs clenched her fingers around the wound on her arm. Dark crimson blood gushed out and stained Zadie's lips a deep scarlet. The thick liquid trickled down the sides of her face and pooled in her tangled hair. A river fell from her mouth, leaving behind a sanguine trail in its wake. The metallic smell of blood filled the air, assaulting their senses.

Zadie's eyes fluttered weakly, her breaths shallow. Yet, as the rich liquid caressed her tongue, a spark of vitality returned. Her wounds, grievous moments before, began to knit together under its miraculous influence.

Above them, the cataclysmic battle waged on. Daimon, in his golden draconic splendor, grappled with the monstrous hybrid, scales clashing against fur and fang. Each strike, each tear of claw and tooth, was a dance of destruction and savagery.

Nadine watched, her emotions a tapestry of worry and wonder, as Zadie's color slowly returned.

"Stay with me," Babs murmured, her tough exterior softened. She had eyes only for Zadie.

The battle raged, a maelstrom of fury. Cricket, with wings outstretched, darted through the chaos, her form a blur against the backdrop of fire and scale.

A growl split the air, a sound laced with a hunger that belonged to nightmares. Sumgal locked his gaze on Cricket, predatory instincts honed by eons of Tiamat's cruel design. With a speed that belied size, he lunged, jaws wide.

"Cricket!" Nadine's scream of warning sliced through the din of combat.

The creature's teeth found purchase, sinking into the delicate membrane of Cricket's wing with sickening ease. The good girl turned warrior let out a heart-wrenching cry as she was wrenched from her flight, her body convulsing in the grip of her assailant. Sumgal shook his head fiercely, a grotesque mimic of a house cat toying with a captured bird.

Nadine scrambled to her feet, her mind racing for a spell, any spell, that could save her sister. But before she could call forth her magic, the adversary sent Cricket tumbling through the air. She landed with a jarring thud atop Nadine, knocking the breath from both of them.

"Are you—" Nadine began, her voice a ragged whisper.

"I'm—I'm all right," Cricket stammered, pain etched in each syllable. "Go. Go finish this."

Gritting her teeth, Nadine pushed herself up, assisting Cricket to a sitting position against a crumbling statue.

Nadine brushed the hair out of Cricket's face and flashed a reassuring smile. "Just stay hidden for now," she said. "Take a moment to catch your breath. I can handle this."

She knew they needed to regroup, to reassess their plan of attack. The monsters born of Tiamat were not mere beasts; they were harbingers of destruction, embodiments of chaos itself. How many of her sisters were still capable of standing, let alone fighting? Cricket and Zadie were out of commission. Daimon seemed wounded but may be able to contribute. It was up to her and Babs now. The fire within Nadine burned hotter, fueled by hope.

CHAPTER 11
ZADIE

Zadie gasped, her lungs drawing breath with a sharp, searing pain that radiated through her chest. Darkness ebbed at the edges of her vision, and she tasted the copper tang of Babs's blood in her mouth—a potent elixir that she felt coursing through her body. Her battered body responded, knitting torn flesh and mending shattered bone, fueled by the life-giving power of her sister's sacrifice.

As she closed her eyes, it felt like a rush of liquid fire running through her veins and capillaries. The intense heat seemed to seek out every cell, purging it of injury and restoring her to a new purest form. But there was more to this sensation than just physical healing—there was an otherworldly power, a primal force that was both mysterious and invigorating. It came from a source completely foreign to her, in no way familiar or instinctual.

For all the physical restoration, a cold spear of dread lodged itself deep within her heart. She was alive, but at what cost? The fear of the unknown clawed at her mind, even as she struggled to rise from the ground where death had briefly claimed her. This didn't feel right. She didn't feel herself. Panic. Her heart raced as she took in her surroundings.

Above her, the sky roiled with the tumult of battle. Nadine, aflame with fury, brandished tongues of fire that lashed out like whips, scorching the night air. Each spell she cast was an act of defiance, a scream of rage against the forces that dared stand between her and her goal.

Zadie tried to sit up, but her body felt weak and foreign. Fear and confusion washed over her, as she realized she was on the side of a battlefield. Memories flooded back and began to fit into place, like puzzle pieces that had been scattered across the floor. She had died — briefly. She scanned the battlefield trying to lay eyes on all her sisters.

Beside Nadine, Daimon — a leviathan of scales and sinew — reared his dragon form high, the iridescent membrane of his wings catching the rising moonlight in a shimmering display of power. Muscles coiled and released as he lunged, talons extended, to grapple with the monstrous abomination that had dared to strike one of their own. His roar was a thunderous cacophony that shook the firmament, echoing the depths from which he hailed. With each movement, he was poetry and destruction intertwined. The sight of him brought a moment of calm to her heart.

Babs's gentle voice floated above Zadie, soothing and calm. "Don't struggle, Zadie. Just stay still. Let the blood heal you." As Zadie's senses returned to her, she could feel Babs's warm hand brushing away the strands of hair that had fallen across her face. She slowly realized that Babs was cradling her in her arms, their bodies nestled in the warm sand beneath them. Gwylm stood over them, shielding Zadie's body completely with his own. The sound of battle filled the air, and Zadie could smell charred wood and burning flesh.

Distress set in. She couldn't just lie here while the fight went on. She needed to help; but her body refused to move. She watched the scene unfold in front of her.

Nadine and Daimon fought as one: the firebrand and the sea-born titan, their strengths complementing each other in a deadly dance. Nadine's flames seared away defenses, exposing chinks in the monster's hide, while Daimon's brute force tore through sinew and scale. It was a spectacle of raw elemental power, a tempest unleashed upon their foe.

The creature, a behemoth born of shadow and malice, reeled under the assault. His mouth uttered curses in a long-forgotten language. His myriad eyes burned with hatred, his maw dripping with venom as he sought to retaliate. With a final, desperate surge, Nadine summoned a column of fire that engulfed the beast, while Daimon's claws found purchase in its heart, rending it asunder.

The monster let out a ghastly howl, a sound that would haunt the dreams of lesser beings, before collapsing into a heap of smoldering flesh and dissipating darkness. The echoes of battle faded into silence, leaving only the ragged breathing of the victors and the crackling of dying flames.

Daimon's eyes flickered to his talons, slick with blood and wrapped tightly around the monstrous heart he had ripped from its owner. He spat crimson droplets from his mouth before tossing the dark organ into the gritty sand below. The heat of battle still pulsed from him, his breath coming in ragged gasps as he stood victorious over their fallen foe. The stench of death and decay filled the air.

With a flash of light and a burst of golden sparks, Daimon transformed from his massive dragon form into a tall, muscular man. His shimmering golden scales slowly receded, morphing into smooth, flawless skin that radiated warmth and power. It was a beautiful sight to behold, as if a myth had come to life before their very eyes. Zadie was unable to tear her gaze away from the magnificent creature who now stood before her.

Daimon ran his fingers through his hair. "Feel the weight of weary triumph. Take a moment; there are more battles to come."

Zadie, still grappling with her rebirth and the fear that gnawed at her gut, watched as Nadine stood triumphant. They were one step closer to their goal. In the aftermath of resurrection and awakening to victory, Zadie willed herself to be ready for the next challenge.

Zadie's limbs quivered as she rose from the ground, her senses sharp as blades. She could hear her own heartbeat, a rapid thunder in her ears. The sound of ever-moving sand whispered to her with each feeble step she took. The grains shifted and danced beneath her feet, creating a soothing melody that seemed to speak to her soul. It was like a gentle lullaby, calming her mind and stirring up dreams newly imagined. She closed her eyes and let herself be carried away by the enchanting rhythm of nature.

As she touched her lips, still tinged with the metallic tang of Babs's blood, she felt an unfamiliar protrusion.

"Zadie? Are you all right?" Cricket's voice was shaded with concern. Her once soaring wings, now tattered and torn, hung limply from her back. That which used to catch the sun's rays and carry her high in the sky were now ragged and lifeless. Each movement caused a sharp wince to spring to her face.

Zadie tried to respond but found her mouth awkward, strange. With tentative fingers, she explored inside, recoiling as they grazed against something sharp. Fangs. Panic clawed at her throat, and she stumbled back, a hand clasping over her mouth.

"Wh-what's happening to me?" Her voice came out garbled, distorted.

"Easy, sister," Nadine soothed, though her eyes betrayed shared anxiety. "It's Babs's blood. It's powerful. You are transformed."

"Transformed?" Zadie spat the word as if it were venom itself. As she gazed down at the pool of melted sand, now transformed into a smooth, shimmering sheet of glass, she caught a glimpse of herself reflected in its surface. The rays of moonlight danced across her features, highlighting the delicate curves of her face and framing her in a soft halo of light. Her reflection was marred by elongated canines that now graced her once familiar smile. A monster. That's what she saw staring back at her, igniting a surge of revulsion within her core.

"Easy there, sis," Babs coaxed.

"Easy?!" Zadie whirled on her sister, her fear morphing into fury. "You've turned me into . . . into this!"

"Zadie, I—" Babs began, but Zadie wasn't finished.

"You knew! You knew what your blood would do!" Zadie's voice cracked as she struggled to keep the newfound feral instincts at bay. Her hands shook, not just from the transformation but from the betrayal she felt puncturing her like a cold blade.

"Zadie, I did it to save you," Babs said, stepping forward. "I was shocked when I turned as well. It took some time for my mind to wrap around this newfound power. But you will come to find it's a wonderful gift. Without my blood, you wouldn't be here. You were—dead."

"Maybe I would have preferred to be dead than, than, to be turned into this!" Zadie's hysterics startled everyone. She felt her control slipping.

"Enough!" Nadine interjected, placing herself between the feuding sisters. "Zadie, your mind will adjust. You are just in shock. Babs did the right thing—you will come to see that and will find gratitude in your heart. Would you really complain about someone loving you enough to not let you die?"

"Gratitude?" Zadie laughed bitterly, her laugh more of a growl. "Fangs do not go with fins!"

Cricket's normally rosy cheeks turned a ghostly white, her voice trembling as she spoke. "I wish I had fangs. I could have saved Gran," she whispered, tears welling up in her eyes.

"Zadie," Babs pleaded, her voice softer now. "Please."

The word hung in the air, the devastated look on Babs's face resonating within Zadie's splintered thoughts.

With a heavy heart, she nodded, swallowing down the rawness of her emotions and the sharpness of her new fangs.

Babs shifted her weight from one foot to the other. "I was shocked and upset when I grew fangs after the challenges, but I am so grateful that the change happened to me. If it hadn't, we would have lost you today. And now, you will be able to save others if you so choose."

Daimon spoke softly. "Zadie, it's kind of hot, you know. The only girl in Atlantis with fangs." He had been observing from a distance. "I'm only one of two in Atlantis that has wings. We can be special together." He shrugged with a smile.

Zadie's voice was flat and lifeless, "I would take wings over fangs."

As the group trudged through the heat-withered foliage, an undercurrent of electricity charged the air. Zadie could feel it prickle her skin, and with every step, the sensation intensified. Her new fangs ached with unfamiliarity, and she fought to keep her mind clear.

Daimon's gait was unsteady, his broad shoulders hunched with pain. The claw marks that marred his flesh wept crimson.

Babs approached him with an offer, her voice a soothing balm. "Daimon, let me heal you."

"Save your strength," Daimon grunted, pushing away her concern. His gaze fixed on the horizon, where the mirage of heat in the moonlight parted just enough to reveal glimpses of an ancient ruin, its stones whispering secrets long forgotten. "We're close. I can sense it—the winter crown is near."

Zadie felt a surge of energy at his words, the importance of their mission thrumming through her like a call to arms. Despite the dread gnawing at her insides, she clenched her fists and prepared for what lay ahead.

The ruins loomed larger as they approached, and with each step, the air grew more humid, the silence deeper. Then, from the heart of the stone circle, a colossal form slithered into view. A seven-headed serpent, its thick scales shimmering, rose before them. Atop one of the creature's heads sat the winter crown, it caught the feeble light and cast eerie shadows.

"Steady," Babs growled, her voice resonating with the authority of a summer princess. Her stance readied, her crown alight with a warm, golden radiance.

Zadie called out, "Cricket, stay back! Nadine, I need you!" Who would have thought that she would come to trust and rely on Nadine?

The menacing hiss of the creature echoed through the ruins, making it seem as though it was emanating from all directions. Its glowing eyes scanned each member of the group with curious appraisal.

Daimon bravely stepped forward, facing the colossal serpent with its seven heads swaying in perfect synchrony. The sheer size of the beast was enough to make one tremble, but Daimon stood his ground. "Vasuki," he called out, his voice unwavering. "We have no quarrel with you. We come not to fight but to return the crown to its rightful realm. Will you give it freely and allow us to depart without conflict?" The air hung heavy with tension as the two powerful forces faced off, their gazes locked in a silent battle of wills. Zadie's heart raced as she awaited Vasuki's response, uncertain of what fate awaited them all in this ancient battleground of beasts and men.

A soft hiss, like a whisper from the shadows, surrounded them all. The voice that spoke was melodic and seductive, weaving its way through the air. "The crown," it purred, "was gifted to our realm. But not without great cost—much bloodshed was spilt in its name." Vasuki's confidence was palpable as she declared, "It is mine now, for I have won it. And the voices that belong to the crown, they wish to remain with me."

A shiver of fear raced through Zadie as she came to the realization that not only was Vasuki wearing the crown, but she had also merged with its formidable power. The golden crown seemed to radiate with its own powerful aura, perched atop her middle head and protected by the fierce guardians on either side—six deadly snake heads, ready to strike at any moment. The colossal body of the serpent loomed over them, a formidable force that seemed to dwarf even Daimon. The seven heads of the snake writhed in a hypnotic rhythm, each one moving independently but somehow in perfect harmony. Its massive body slithered and undulated, creating a mesmerizing and terrifying display that left Zadie frozen in fear.

A palpable, dangerous energy crackled and sizzled in the air, a clear indication that powerful winter magic was being wielded in this forgotten realm. Zadie's senses were on high alert as she scanned her surroundings, wondering how the ancient magical forces had been altered and what potential dangers lay ahead. The very atmosphere seemed to vibrate with raw power.

Her eyes widened in awe as she watched Daimon's transformation, his body growing and shifting until he was a massive dragon. His once smooth bronze skin was now covered in shimmering golden scales, reflecting the moonlight that peeked through the clouds above. The garnet at his chest glowed with an otherworldly intensity, pulsating with power and strength. His talons dug deep into the warm sand, poised and ready to take flight into the open sky.

The battle erupted with a ferocious rage. The serpent's hiss echoed through the air, each of her multiple voices a symphony of malice and raw power. With swift movements, she lunged at the sisters, her many heads bobbing and weaving in a deadly dance. Their graceful forms darted and weaved in response to the snapping jaws and lashing tongues that threatened to overtake them. Each strike was fueled by their unwavering drive to defeat this ancient creature.

Together, they fought with a synchronicity born of blood and bond. Nadine, her rage a living thing, summoned gales of fire that howled with ferocity, buffeting the beast and giving them precious moments to strike.

And Zadie—Zadie moved with a speed and cantor that startled even herself. With each thrust and parry of her knife, she channeled this new primal power into her blows, her increased strength lending her strikes a vicious edge.

"Keep Vasuki distracted!" Babs shouted, her fingers weaving intricate patterns in the air as she prepared a spell that crackled with the essence of the earth.

As if sensing peril, the serpent reared back, her crowning head poised to unleash devastation upon them. But Zadie was faster, her body driven by an unstoppable will. She lunged forward, her blade singing through the air, and with a scream that melded victory and desperation, she struck true.

The head with the crown fell, severed from its body, the winter crown tumbling from its perch and landing with a thud that seemed to shake the very foundations of this world. The sisters stood still amidst the carnage of this small triumph.

Zadie's heart pounded in her chest, her hands trembling as she stared at the artifact that had cost them so much. The winter crown, the key to their father's freedom, lay within reach, and yet a strange foreboding settled over her.

Zadie's fingers closed around the winter crown, its icy filigree biting into her flesh as a surge of chaos magic raced through her very being. It felt as though Babs's potent blood had awakened something ancient and formidable within her—a power that was both exhilarating and terrifying. Her body thrummed with newfound strength, her senses heightened to an almost unbearable degree.

"Zadie!" Babs shouted, her voice laced with urgency and awe.

But Zadie barely heard her. The world around her pulsed with vibrant colors and sounds, each one magnified by the chaos that now flooded her being. She turned to face the remaining heads of the serpent, her eyes ablaze with ferocious intent.

A wild, primal cry erupted from her throat, unleashing a siren's call that had never been heard before. Her voice carried with it a powerful surge of raw magic, a maelstrom of light and shadow that whipped through the air with ferocity. The wounded beast cowered in fear as the maelstrom approached, unable to withstand the overwhelming power. Her sisters gasped in awe and terror at the display of otherworldly strength and ferocity.

The serpent coiled and thrashed, Vasuki's remaining heads shrieking in unison as the powerful magic engulfed them. The air crackled with energy, and sparks of light danced around the creature's writhing body. With a blinding flash, the last remnants of the beast disintegrated into nothing but dust. Zadie stood amidst the ruins, her chest heaving with exertion and exhilaration. In her trembling hand, she held the winter crown, its icy glow illuminating her triumphant expression. She had vanquished the formidable serpent and claimed the crown as their own.

As the rush of battle faded, the significance of their victory settled upon her like a mantle. They had retrieved the winter crown, a symbol of immense power and authority within the fae courts. It was the key to their father's release from the icy grasp of the winter king, a bargaining chip that carried with it the weight of centuries-old politics and the promise of freedom.

Babs approached cautiously. "We did it," she breathed, her brown eyes reflecting the mixture of triumph and trepidation that they all felt.

"Finally," Nadine murmured. "Zadie, that was amazing." Nadine's gaze locked on the crown in Zadie's hand,

and a smile grew across her face. "Let's go. The king will part with our father easily, once his precious crown is returned."

The debris of the chaotic battlefield lay scattered like a macabre tapestry across the barren ground. Zadie, her breaths shallow and rapid, stood amidst the ruins, the winter crown heavy in her trembling hands. She scanned the aftermath, noting the way her sisters moved with weary precision, their faces etched with the exhaustion of victory hard-won.

Cricket nodded. "You all right, Zadie?" she asked, fatigue marking her features. "I've never seen you use your power for harm."

Daimon's tall figure was silhouetted against the smoldering ruins, his expression a mixture of exhaustion and grief as he gazed down at the monstrous corpse. His features were drawn and shadowed with weariness. The scales of the monster's green skin were dull and lifeless. Daimon's stance was still and somber, as if paying respect to a fallen foe.

Zadie's hand trembled as she ran it across her furrowed brow, leaving streaks of sweat and grime in its wake. She could feel the heat of exhaustion radiating off her skin, and a pounding headache threatened to overtake her senses. "I'm feeling quite unwell," she murmured, her voice strained and weak.

A slight distance away, Babs stood apart from the group, her shoulders tense. The agitation emanating from her was palpable, even without the bond of blood that linked them. Zadie's gaze lingered on her sister, sensing a storm brewing beneath the surface of Babs's impenetrable composure.

As her sisters prepared to depart, Zadie's thoughts drifted unbidden to the life that awaited her in Atlantis. She was already committed to abandoning the human world, abandoning Tom, accustomed to the physical ache within her chest—a wound that no amount of magic could heal.

Two new fangs, sharp and deadly, remained hidden behind her parted lips. These were the physical manifestation of the irreversible transformation she had undergone, a perceivable symbol of the power she now possessed. But it was not death that she should wrought with these fangs; they were meant to grant the gift of life. Her very blood should be a gift. As she stood there, still trembling from the surge of magic that had just rushed through her body, she marveled at the fullness of emotion that had consumed her. A storm of rage had roiled within her, fierce and unrelenting like a hurricane, and she had unleashed it without hesitation or remorse. This was the new strength that lay within her, waiting to be tapped into at any given moment.

The notion of permanence settled heavily upon her, even as chaos magic still hummed under her skin, a foreign entity that surged through her with every beat of her heart. How could she reconcile these changes with the girl who once swam carefree through the ocean's depths? The girl who laughed easily and dreamed of a simple future now seemed like a distant memory, an echo of a life that could never be reclaimed. She had just killed a monster. Killed. That wasn't who she was. She calmed. She charmed. She loved. Not—killed.

"Zadie?" Cricket's voice cut through her reverie, gentle but insistent. "Are you ready to head back?"

Zadie replied, though her voice lacked its usual buoyancy. "As ready as I can be." With a final glance at Babs, whose own eyes held a torrent of unspoken thoughts, Zadie shook her head, clearing her thoughts.

"Zadie," came a voice, smooth and as comforting as the ebb and flow of the tides.

She turned to find Daimon standing behind her, his dragon form melting away to reveal the tall, lithe figure of the Mer she knew. His eyes, returning to the color of ocean storms, regarded her with an intensity that made her newly sensitive skin tingle.

"Your transformation," he started, stepping closer, "it was . . . unexpected."

"Tell me about it," she murmured, her voice a low hum marred by the unfamiliar weight of her fangs.

He reached out, tracing the contours of her face with a gentleness that belied his warrior's strength. "Unexpected, yes, but you are still beautiful, Zadie—fangs and all."

A wry smile flickered across her lips, even as her heart skipped a beat. She hadn't expected such tenderness from him, they had only just met. But the softness in his eyes, the careful touch of his hand—it spoke of a connection that was as bewildering as it was undeniable.

"Beautiful doesn't quite feel like the word for it," she said, her voice barely above a whisper. "I feel powerful, dangerous even. I'm beginning to understand Babs a little bit more. Her magic—it's like having a storm brewing inside." She rung her hands. "I'm not sure how to be this new version of myself."

"Beauty can be dangerous," Daimon replied, his thumb tracing the line of her jaw. "And power does not diminish your grace. It adds to it, if you wield it correctly."

Their eyes locked, and for a moment, the world around them seemed to fall away. The battles fought, the crown won, the future uncertain—all of it receded under the quiet of the moment they shared.

But as quickly as it came, the sensation vanished. Zadie's head swam, her knees buckled, and she grasped Daimon's arm for support.

"Zadie?" Concern laced his voice as he steadied her.

"Something's not right," she gasped, the disorientation clawing at her consciousness. Her eyes sought out Babs, who stood apart, her posture rigid, her expression unreadable. Zadie could sense a foreign magic seize her sister. The smell of bog, damp and wet, assaulted her senses.

"Babs, why?" Zadie whispered, the question hanging in the air, fraught with a sense of looming dread that threatened to betray them all.

CHAPTER 12
BABS

Sand spray danced like restless spirits in the realm that hung suspended between the embrace of wind and the caress of shadow. Babs's gaze, sharp as the edges of the crown she bore, locked onto Zadie's sea-glass eyes, an unspoken apology whispering through the searing air before she snatched the winter crown from Zadie's slender hands.

Babs's voice caught in her throat like sharp shards of glass as she whispered, "I'm sorry." The words were heavy with regret and remorse, as if they carried the weight of the world on them. She could feel the jagged edges cutting into her insides, leaving behind a trail of pain and sorrow. Her breaths came out shaky and uneven, like a broken record playing on repeat. It was a small phrase, but it held so much emotion that it seemed to echo through the air, lingering long after it was spoken.

The heavy weight of her sisters' unspoken worries bore down on her, their scrutinizing gazes like hot lasers infiltrating her being. Their expressions were a tumultuous mix of confusion and concern, like waves colliding against the shore. She could feel their doubts and fears radiating off of them in palpable waves, making her stomach flip with unease.

With the prize grasped, an intolerable cold seeped into her fingers. The summer diadem settled upon her head whispered, a cacophony of voices both discordant and desperate. They emanated from within the roughly carved bone of the princesses before her, clawing at her mind, urging, pleading — *"Call to Liande."*

"This is the moment; this is our chance."

"Hurry, lest you falter."

"Call to Liande — the time is now."

"Away from here — quickly."

"This is best."

The voices clambered over one another. All in agreement. She was in agreement.

Gwylm's deep voice shouted in her mind. *"Is this our true path? The sacrifice could be great."* His gaze lingered from one sister to the other.

Undeterred, Babs traced the glyphs etched into her arm, their glow pulsating like the heartbeat of the earth itself. In her mind's eye, the visage of Liande emerged, as clear as if she stood before her. "Reach out to me," Babs commanded, her voice threaded with the authority of her royal status. "Bring me to your side. I have the crown." She ran her fingers over the twisted metal, confirming to herself that indeed — she had won."

Nadine's question shattered the fragile silence, tentative and quiet. "Babs, what are you doing?" Her twin's face twisted in horror, her eyes gleaming with the reality of betrayal.

A surge of magic enclosed Babs and Gwylm, a maelstrom of energy swirling about them — a bubble impenetrable by sister or beast. Daimon, magnificent in his dragon form, charged against the barrier, his claws futile against the invisible shield.

The world contorted, reality bending to the will of the summer princess, as she followed the threads that brought her and Gwylm to Liande's presence. They were pulled through space and time, their beings melding with the mystical force around them. They landed with a thud beside Liande's pool, nestled within the heart of the bog where languid alligators slid through murky waters, their eyes glinting with ancient knowledge. Above, Liande's ghost army wailed, their cries suspended between worlds, yearning for release.

Liande's laughter pierced the humid air, maniacal and triumphant. With hands that held the fate of seasons, she relieved Babs of the crown, her eyes gleaming with dark delight. "Well done," Liande praised, the promise of reward lacing her words like the sweetest poison. "We shall be recompensed in kind."

The stillness hung heavily in the air, mirroring the weight of Babs's decision. The humid atmosphere seemed to smother her, but she knew there was no going back now. She had chosen her path, one lined with ambition and built on betrayal. However, in the cutthroat world of the courts, only the most cunning would emerge the victor.

Gwylm leisurely strolled toward the closest cluster of trees, staying clear of the pond.

The air around Liande shimmered and thrummed as she lifted her arms, a serpentine grace in her movements that amplified the grave incantation upon her lips. The symbols etched into her scaled hide glowed with an eerie light, casting rippling shadows across the bog. Babs was mesmerized as she witnessed the raw power emanating from Liande, a rushing stream of ancient magic channeled through the earth, then spread out beyond.

"By Inanna's will," Liande's voice echoed, a sonorous chant that swelled and dipped like the flight of a raven. "I call forth the winter king, keeper of the longest night."

As if in response to Liande's summons, the balmy air grew chill, and the sun-dappled sky curdled into a brooding overcast. Dark clouds roiled overhead, and the placid waters of the pool began to churn, mud swirling in dizzying patterns. A sense of foreboding gripped Babs's heart—the quiet before the storm.

With a crack like thunder rending the heavens, the center of the pool erupted in a maelstrom of ice and shadow. From this tumultuous birth, the winter king emerged, his majestic form cutting through the darkness, razor-sharp wings of icicles outstretched as he soared into the dimmed sky. Behind him, a host of winter fae soldiers took flight, their armor glinting coldly, their eyes alight and alert.

"I honor your summons, Daughter of Inanna," the winter king intoned, his voice as deep and unyielding as the glaciers of his realm. He descended, settling on the ground with a regal poise. His eyes flickered to Liande's hands. A smile cut across his face as he extended a hand toward Liande, who bowed her head and presented the crown.

"At last," he said as he took the artifact, its jewels gleaming with captured frost. "The snow queen will be overjoyed. Winter has much to celebrate." A ripple of acknowledgment ripped through his men. With a gesture both grand and intimate, the king's magic unfurled like a winter bloom, enshrouding Liande in a cocoon of pale light. "Your loyalty is not forgotten."

Babs witnessed the transformation with bated breath — a reversal of curses.

As Liande's scaly exterior receded, revealing the flawless and fair skin underneath, her once cold and monstrous appearance transformed into one of regal beauty. Her chiseled features gave her an otherworldly allure, sharp and defined like the edges of a precious gemstone. Covered in nothing but a see-through shift, her form was a striking contrast to the gnarled trees and murky waters surrounding them. Sabella's curse was broken, and the balance of power shifted palpably in the air.

The winter king's voice cut through the silence as he declared, "I shall stand witness for you at the summer court." He cleared his throat. "I will ensure the opportunity to dethrone Sabella without intrusion or trickery. You shall secure rightful rule."

Liande's laughter rang out, clear and victorious. She raised her hands, turning them over, marveling at their youthful beauty. "Thank you, my lord," she murmured, waves of relief washing over her face. "By day's end," she proclaimed, turning to Babs with a gaze fierce and exultant, "we shall reign supreme over summer's domain."

"Indeed, summer will be ours," Babs affirmed, her voice steady despite the whirlwind of emotions within. She stood tall beside Liande, united in ambition, ready to face whatever storms their actions might unleash upon all the worlds.

With the crown now seated in the winter king's grasp, she stepped forward, her feet sinking into the soft, murky ground of the bog, her purpose as firm as the earth she commanded.

Her eyes pleaded and voice trembled. "Your Majesty," Babs began, "now that our alliance is sealed, I have one more request. My father—please, release him from your realm and allow him to be reunited with my mother. Allow them to live out their days in the mortal realm." Her words hung heavy, encased in the silence that followed.

The winter king, clad in frost and majesty, turned his gaze upon her. His eyes, glacial and fierce, seemed to see right through her, reading her desperation. He cocked his head, a gesture that carried the weight of eons, and his voice resonated with the chill of winter's breath.

"Was it Nadine who brought me this crown?" he mused aloud, as if sifting through his thoughts like snowflakes caught in the wind. "No, I do not see her here. And was it you, Babs of the Culebra line, summer princess, who fulfilled our bargain? No, it was not."

His words fell like icicles, sharp and unyielding. "Your father remains mine to do with as I please, and Nadine, having failed the task set before her, will be called back to winter. That was the deal struck, and deals, as you know, are sacred among us."

Babs clenched her jaw, her brown eyes smoldering with an inner fire that belied her earthy nature. "Surely, you have no need of either of them," she pressed, the plea wrapped in a veneer of confidence. "Why not grant this one concession? This mercy?"

The air around them hummed with magic, thick with the scent of impending change.

"Deals made cannot be undone on mere whims, or honored when not fulfilled," the winter king replied, his tone final, dismissing her entreaty.

Babs knew the truth of his words; the ancient magics were not to be trifled with. Yet there was something in his demeanor—a flicker of curiosity, perhaps—that suggested the door had not been fully closed. For now, she would have to bide her time, holding on to the sliver of possibility that her father and sister might yet be freed.

She bowed her head in reluctant acknowledgment. As the winter king turned away, his soldiers forming a spectral guard behind him, Babs's mind whirred with plans. Brute force would be inviting death with the king; perhaps cunning and strategy could work. Patience. She would have to have patience.

The game of crowns played by the fae was intricate and deadly, and Babs intended to emerge victorious.

The winter king paused and turned back toward Babs, frost rimming his severe blue eyes as he weighed her plea for a moment longer. Then, with the subtlest of nods, he pronounced, "We will speak of it later. Perhaps someday I will have need of the summer princess. On that day, we will barter."

With that cryptic promise hanging in the air, he turned toward the pool. The surface shimmered, reflecting a sky that no longer held the warmth of a peaceful night but heralded the burden of rolling clouds that threatened release. With an imperious wave of his hand, the water erupted into a swirling vortex, tendrils of mist spiraling into the gathering darkness above.

The winter king stepped forward, the hem of his frosted cloak brushing against the ground, caressing the earth itself. He paused at the edge of the pool, glancing back over his shoulder with an inscrutable expression.

"We meet at the summer court, come dawn." He plunged into the maelstrom, his form dissolving into silvery shards that disappeared beneath the roiling surface. One by one, his men followed, their armored forms becoming ghostly apparitions before vanishing altogether. In moments, the pool stilled.

Babs stood motionless, her fists clenched at her sides, the power of the summer princess crown pulsating against her brow. Anger seared through her face, hot and bitter, as she turned to face Liande, who watched the king's exit with an unreadable expression.

"Your assurances were empty," Babs hissed, her words laced with venom. "My father languishes in chains because of the bargain you struck. And what? Am I to wait upon the whims and desires of a frost-hearted king?"

Liande's eyes, dark pools reflecting eons of cunning, met hers unflinchingly. "Patience, dear Babs," she murmured, her voice smooth as the slick mud beneath their feet. "The courts move in cycles and seasons. Timing is everything."

"Patience?" Babs spat the word like a curse. She knew Liande's words were true; she had come to the same conclusion. But she needed to release the anger bubbling up inside. "While my father suffers, we are to play sycophants to a ruler draped in snow? I think not. You promised me my father's freedom, Liande. You swore it on the old magics. Do your words hold no weight?"

"Everything will come to pass in due time," Liande purred, her voice a sultry mix of desire and command. She ran her tongue along her luscious lips, relishing the new sensation. "Remember our alliance, Babs. Our union of power will bring forth a new era. All you desire shall be within your grasp once Sabella's reign ends."

"Desire?" Babs's laughter was bitter and lacking any joy. It had been a while since she genuinely laughed with happiness. Everything had been difficult for such a long time. "What use have I for desire when my honor and the love of my family are at stake? You deal in shadows and whispers, Liande. But know this—the light of summer burns even in the darkest of shadows. And I will see my father freed—and Nadine—with or without your help. I will not lose my sisters over this."

Liande's lips curved into a seductive smile, her eyes locking onto her protege with an alluring gaze. She trailed her fingers sensually over her sheer shift. Her eyes closed as she relished the feel of her own smooth, delicate skin. "Bold words, Princess of Summer. But boldness alone does not win wars. Strategy, foresight, and—yes—patience, are the weapons we must wield. Trust in the path we have chosen, for it leads to victory."

Babs's heart hammered against her rib cage, a drumbeat calling her to action. Yet she knew Liande spoke a twisted truth. The game they played was long, and each piece moved upon the board bore consequences far-reaching and profound.

"Then let us hope," Babs said, her mind hardening like roots digging deep into the earth, "that the fruits of our patience do not wither on the vine."

Liande nodded once, sharply, her eyes glinting with a challenge of their own. "They shall not, Babs. On that, you have my word."

And in the shadowy realm of the fae, where words bound tighter than iron chains, such promises were not given lightly.

Liande's fingers traced the enigmatic symbols etched upon her arm, their ethereal glow mirrored on Babs's own skin. A silent vow passed between them, an intimate sharing of power that bound their fates together. "When I ascend to my rightful throne, you shall want for nothing," Liande whispered, her voice an enchantress's's call wrapped in velvet. "Choose your heart's desire, and it shall be yours."

Liande took a step back, her tongue licking her top lip, slow and languid. "How do you like my real form? My true glamour?" Her umber eyes burned bright with desire. Her movements were sensual as she slowly roved her hands over her chest and brazenly touched herself. The thin wet material of her shift clung to her every curve, showing her bodies ready response. Babs couldn't take her eyes from her, mesmerized by the blatant pleasure on display. She recalled the searing image of Liande, commanding the winter king to satisfy her with coarse pleasure as they sealed their pact all that time ago. The memory of Liande's raw passion and, in a strange way, dominance over the winter king stirred a fire within Babs.

That was Liande in her cursed form. This was Liande in all her beauty, reborn. Babs felt her mouth salivate. As if reading Babs's mind, Liande spread her legs wide and trailed one hand down the length of her torso and rubbed slow and luxuriously, giving herself pleasure. A moan escaped her parted crimson lips, a temptresses sound to Babs's ears.

Babs surrendered to the welcoming temptation. She closed the distance between them, nipping at that welcoming mouth. Every brush of Liande's soft fingertips against her skin was a spark igniting wildfires across her senses. Babs yielded to the tempestuous waves of pleasure. She reveled in the contrast—Liande's touch tender where once talons reigned, the caress of her long hair a silken promise against Babs's fevered flesh.

"Your gentleness . . . it is not necessary," Babs murmured, her breath hitching as she spoke. Their gazes locked, a smoldering challenge passing unspoken.

"Is force what you seek?" Liande's voice was low, a growl of promise that sent shivers rippling over Babs's skin.

Without another word, Liande's actions became a tempest, her movements embodying the ferocity of her primal longings. With haste born of urgency, she divested Babs of her garments, leaving her exposed to the elements and to the fervor in Liande's eyes.

Babs was laid bare upon the sodden earth, the coolness of the mud silky against her heated skin.

Liande, with predatory grace, dropped to her knees and began to crawl toward Babs, each movement calculated and purposeful. Her eyes gleamed with hunger, like a lioness stalking her prey. With a rough grip, she parted Babs's legs, leaving red marks where her fingers dug into the skin. Mud dripped from Liande's hands as she held on to Babs tightly. "Do you offer yourself?" she asked in a low, dangerous voice.

Babs's body thrummed with aching need, every nerve ending pulsing for Liande's touch. The heat between her legs burned brighter, fueling her wild desire. She could almost taste the sweet release that Liane's touch would bring, like a tantalizing promise just out of reach. Every inch of her skin tingled with need, yearning. Her urge was building within her, ready to be unleashed by Liande's skilled hands and lips.

"Please," Babs gasped.

Liande, slowly, descended between her thighs, her tongue a wild entity all its own. The world narrowed to the electric touch, the rush of air from Babs's lungs as her back arched in involuntary supplication, shoulders imprinting into the forgiving ground.

"I will take all you are willing to give," Liande declared, her words a vow and a claim, spoken to the rhythm of Babs's gasps. And in that moment, amidst the murk and mire of the bog, Babs realized the depth of their entanglement—how closely pleasure and power were intertwined in the dance of their union.

CHAPTER 13
NADINE

The revelation struck like a tidal wave, leaving Nadine adrift in shock. Babs had vanished with the crown.

Babs.

Vanished.

With the crown.

"Impossible." Daimon's voice was barely audible amidst the howling winds that swept through the barren in-between lands. His brow furrowed in confusion as he spoke. "The failed timelines are separate from our own existence, our own worlds. But if she managed to tear a hole in this reality and link it to ours, it could leave a trace, a pattern for something to sneak through." He raked his hands through his hair in distress. "This is not good. Not good at all."

Zadie hunched her shoulders, as if shielding her heart. Nadine's eyes widened in surprise at Zadie's new appearance. The blood of Babs had not only healed Zadie's wounds and given her fangs, but it had also subtly altered her features to resemble Babs more closely. Could it be that Babs had transferred more than just her healing abilities?

Nadine couldn't make sense of it. She allowed her eyes to unfocus, her consciousness to expand beyond the physical realm, bisecting time and space as she tapped into her connection with the winter court—the winter king to be precise.

Her life had changed with a summons to appear before the court, with the king demanding she find and return his missing crown. After being held captive for what felt like an eternity, she finally had a chance to show her worth and negotiate for the one thing she wanted most—freedom for herself and her father.

Why the king thought she would succeed when her mother had failed was beyond her understanding. From what she could piece together, she suspected that her family was actually working against the winter court. But she was ready for the challenge. She would succeed where others had failed.

She had boldly asked for her reward, masking her true emotions with a confident demeanor. But her quick wit proved to be no match for the winter king. He had viciously marked her as his possession, like a dog urinating on his territory, before allowing her to accompany him to the summer court. Her humiliation had been carried out in front of all to see. True, it was the old way of binding a pact. She should have known it would be a part of the bargain. Yet it brought fire to her cheeks, just in the remembering.

That was not the first time she had been used in such a manner. Many nights, she had partaken—willingly—in the endless drunken evenings where lust demanded to be quenched, not caring from whom. She reveled in the scent of alcohol and sweat lingering on her skin. It was faceless, carnal, rutting. Each passing from one partner to another, a physical dream that they all languished in. A nightmarish world that left her body covered in a tapestry of pain and pleasure.

But this had not been about passion or need. There was no mutual give and take. He only took, displaying his authority as all watched on. She had been expected to act appreciative. Honored, even. She had swallowed her feelings then, as she did now. Her face a mask.

She pressed her hand firmly against her flat belly, feeling the life growing inside — an unplanned result of his sovereignty. In the end, she had taken — and kept. She fixated on the tiny heartbeat, a blend of herself and him. With each beat, she felt a deeper connection to the child. In her mind's eye, she saw a strand of light connecting her to the child, stretching out endlessly until she saw . . . him.

He ascended gracefully above the swirling pool in the throne room of the summer court, a fierce, cold figure surrounded by his loyal men. Their wings, vibrant with color and power, stretched out in unison and beat against the air, creating a whirlwind of gusts that stirred up the crystal-clear water below.

At the king's right drifted Ambrosias, the winter prince, exuding a mesmerizing aura of raw power and seduction. His regal form hovered over the space, commanding attention. A crown, mirroring his father's, graced his head. In his hand, he tightly gripped the object of her failed task, the price for her freedom. Nadine's stomach churned with sickness as she caught sight of her sister Babs on the shore below, her wolf sitting by her feet at attention.

Standing before her was a magnificent fae creature, her otherworldly aura pulsing with an intense and dangerous energy. A seething mass of tormented spirits swirled around her, emanating an ambiance of agony and destruction, as if they were ready to possess and destroy anyone who dared to cross the fae's path.

"Babs and the crown . . . they are at the summer court." Nadine found her voice raspy. It was difficult to speak while in vision. "She has already handed the crown over."

Zadie's eyes drooped with exhaustion as she said, "Nadine, I didn't know you were a seer."

Nadine shook the vision from her mind and took several cleansing breaths. "When I have a connection, yes, I can see."

Cricket pressed. "Like your connection with Babs?"

Nadine let out a deep sigh, her voice filled with exhaustion. "I used to be constantly connected to Babs. But lately, something has changed. I can't always reach her." She couldn't shake the image of the fae woman she saw in her vision, standing close to Babs. A sense of dread tugged at her heart.

"I fear the crown's return is about to set a battle in motion. This has ceased to be about our father's fate, or mine, for that matter. This is now about the fate of the courts — the future hangs precariously in the balance."

Daimon's jaw tightened as he spoke. "What ruin have you brought to the gates of Atlantis?" He began to pace back and forth, leaving dust clouds in his wake.

Cricket took Nadine's hand gently, her eyes pleading as she asked, "Can you see? Is Babs okay?" Worry lined her face.

"You will see for yourself," Daimon's voice boomed. "I will fly us back to the portal." With scarcely a nod, he unfurled into his true draconic form — a colossal beast of shimmering crimson scales, each one reflecting the turmoil of the in-between lands like fractured shards of reality. The transformation rippled through him, muscles expanding and bones stretching until he towered above them, a leviathan born of sea and sky. He lowered his long neck, inviting them to climb upon his thick hide.

Cricket extended a trembling hand and traced her fingers over his shimmering scales.

Her face lit up with appreciation. "It's like polished amber," she mused. With a gentle nudge, the dragon offered his back for her to mount. She spread her iridescent wings and attempted to fly, but finding her wings too damaged she chose to climb up his side sit gracefully at the curve of his neck. Nadine hesitated for only a moment before following suit. She climbed up the living mountain that was Daimon, carefully finding secure footholds between the ridges of his vast spine. Zadie joined them, her slender frame standing out against the dragon's immense size as she nestled in behind Nadine.

With a powerful downbeat of his wings, they took flight, soaring above the endless expanse of desolate white that once threatened to consume them whole. Below, the barren land slowly morphed into an eerie landscape, with dry riverbeds and towering spires of jagged rocks jutting out like gnarled fingers. It was a world forgotten by time, abandoned and left to decay, a tapestry of death, painted onto the silent canvas of a forgotten world. Nadine's sharp gaze caught a glimpse of a dark edifice carved into the barren cliffs, its jagged spires reaching out like clawed fingers grasping for relief. "What secrets do you hold?" she murmured, more to herself than her companions.

Nadine was at a loss as to what they would find when they reached the summer court. Had Babs struck a deal with the winter king? Having already delivered the crown, the king would not be bound to fulfill the deal he had made with Nadine. What could be more important to Babs than freeing her father? Freeing her? How could Babs do this to her? She couldn't make sense of it all.

Maj and Ashur, their figures hazy through the wind-swept vista, stood sentinel over the portal — a shimmering doorway holding firm against the encroaching entropy of the failed timeline.

Cricket alighted first, her form slipping through the portal with a grace that belied the exhaustion of their quest. Nadine, poised to follow, cast one last glance over her shoulder, a premonition prickling at the edge of her consciousness.

In a sudden and terrifying moment, the sand beneath Zadie's feet erupted in a violent burst. It was like a gaping mouth of golden grains, hungrily swallowing her whole as she screamed in terror. The sand shifted and churned like a living being, revealing the grotesque creature lurking just below its surface. Its muscular body resembled that of a man, but with scorpion-like features that were both hor-rifying and intriguing at the same time. Its long, barbed tail flicked out with savage intent, snatching up Zadie in its pincers before disappearing back into the depths of the treacherous sand. Her cries were muffled by the swirling grains as they consumed her.

Trapped between two states of being, Daimon let out a guttural scream of fury. He clawed at the shifting sand, desperately trying to dig his way to Zadie. But the sand seemed to have a mind of its own, contorting and slithering away from his grasp. It was as if the very ground were alive, taunting him and holding Zadie captive with its magical barrier. Daimon's rage only grew as he realized there was no way through, no way to save her.

Nadine's heart froze in terror as she saw her sister Za-die in peril once again — all because of her. She summoned every ounce of tenacity and anger, channeling it into her flaming hands as she desperately tried to break through the shifting prison encasing Zadie. But her fiery rage turned the gritty sand beneath her into a molten pool, transforming it into sharp shards of glass that only served to further seal her sister from her reach.

The betrayal of Babs only added to her pain and guilt, as she imagined her father imprisoned for eternity because of her failure.

Her failure.

Her failure.

With a searing glare at the world around her, Nadine let out a primal scream fueled by self-loathing and hopelessness. Years of pent-up emotions were released in one agonizing scream as she fell to her knees, hot tears streaming down her face.

Daimon's draconian form dissipated like smoke caught in a gale, his massive wings folding into the fabric of humanity as he struggled to regain his human shape. Nadine's heart hammered against her chest, each beat echoing the dread that clawed at her insides.

Daimon's voice was rough with emotion. "This landscape is a cage. We have not the power to unbind it." His face was drained of color.

Nadine's heart hammered against her chest, each beat echoing the dread that clawed at her insides.

She was worthless.

She was a failure.

She was nothing.

Nadine urged, her voice hoarse with sorrow as she seized Daimon's hand, "Come on!" Without a backward glance, she dragged him toward the shimmering portal. Their footsteps sank in the sandy ground.

The portal flickered like a candle threatened by the wind,

its light waning under the weight of the somber sky. Maj, slumped yet resolute, her hands outstretched, sustained the gateway through sheer force of will. But as Nadine and Daimon crossed the threshold, a tremor tore through Maj's frame — a harbinger of her impending collapse.

The portal convulsed violently, the edges curling inward as if devouring itself. A final glimpse of the failed timeline — their last hope for Zadie — vanished behind them, swallowed by the void. The portal snapped shut with an ominous finality.

Maj's legs buckled, and she fell like a great oak succumbing to a relentless axe. Ashur, swift as a summer storm, caught her before she fell to the ground. Cradling her unconscious form, he whispered endearments that were lost amidst the din of chaos.

"Stay with me, Maj," Ashur implored, his voice a soothing balm. Her eyelids fluttered, the battle-hardened Mer fighting the pull of darkness that beckoned her to surrender to exhaustion. With a smile, Ashur teased, "I thought I was the only one that made you swoon."

Nadine observed the scene. Guilt gnawed at her for leading them all into this maelstrom. Gran was dead. Zadie taken from them. Babs a traitor. What did she have left? Who did she have left? She placed a hand on her midsection.

"Mama," she whispered to herself. She wanted Mama.

As her gaze fell upon Cricket, Nadine noticed the large tear-filled eyes staring back at her. Cricket's lips quivered uncontrollably, a telltale sign of her overwhelming emotions. Nadine felt sobs rise up in her own body, threatening to consume her. She struggled to regulate her breathing, but the moment was too much to bear. She was suffocating under the weight of failure.

I failed.

I failed.

I failed.

As panic engulfed Nadine, she clung to Cricket like a lifeline. Cricket's tender touch engulfed Nadine, and her murmured words felt like a warm balm on her wounds. The scent of honeysuckle and jasmine filled the air, as Cricket gently guided Nadine down to the ground and rocked her as if she were a child. Nadine had never experienced such gentleness before. With each gentle sway, Nadine let out all the sobs she had pushed down. She cried an ocean's worth of tears. Cricket whispered, "We will fix this, you and I."

We.

A word so foreign to Nadine, and yet its force was as powerful as the sun. Nadine tentatively stuttered, "Do you—do you mean it?"

Cricket pulled her tight, her arms warm and kind. "Of course. We are sisters."

Hot tears streamed down Nadine's face. Her chest contracted, the pressure as heavy as if an elephant had sat upon her. For years—years—Zadie and Cricket denied that Nadine was alive. They refused to believe Babs. And when Nadine had come back, they had not accepted her. They were hesitant.

But Cricket.

Cricket had just said.

Finally said.

They were sisters.

Daimon's voice snapped Nadine out of her thoughts, his tone a rugged contrast to his usual playful banter. "We must return for Zadie!"

Nadine had no idea how to save Zadie. But she could see a path to helping Cricket claim her rightful place as winter princess. Hadn't she heard someone refer to Cricket as the light bearer? And Babs the balancer? Nadine could feel it in her bones — they needed to get to the summer court, right now. She countered Daimon's statement, her eyes rimmed red. "Ashur, tell me you have a portal to the summer court."

The air swirled around Ashur pulsing with power, his expression grave. "I can send you there," he confirmed. "But it's one way. Once you step through, there's no return."

Cricket's face paled. "We can't abandon her. Zadie's alone, trapped."

"Cricket," Nadine implored, tightening her embrace. "Madness is being unleashed between the two courts. I fear you have a part to play in all this. Ambrosias awaits to place the crown upon your head. I saw it in his grasp." Nadine stood and reached a hand out to help Cricket rise to her feet. "Perhaps all is not lost. If you wear the crown, you will have the power to send Father and me back home to Mama. And" — Nadine choked on the words — "together we will help figure out what bind Babs has gotten herself into to have chosen to betray us so."

Cricket's lower lip trembled. She turned and searched Daimon's eyes, seeking the assurance she so desperately needed.

"I know very little of the courts above, I leave that to you to figure out. Upon Tiamat's ancient might, I swear I will return Zadie to our world, or die trying." Daimon's oath was a solemn vow.

Cricket hesitated, but ultimately gave in with a nod. Daimon stepped forward, carefully taking Maj's limp form from Ashur's grasp.

"You've tarried too long within the fractured realms," Ashur said, his tone laced with concern as he addressed

Daimon. "It has exacted its toll on Maj." His gaze lingered on her serene face, then shifted back to Daimon with a heavy heart. "I see you are not untouched by its cost."

Daimon's jaw tightened, understanding the unspoken truth between brothers. Time spent in the in-between had drained them more than they dared admit. He cradled Maj in his arms, her head resting against his chest. Ashur hovered close, his expression a mix of concern and solemnity as he ran a finger gently over Maj's pale cheek. Her normally vibrant eyes were closed, her breathing shallow but even.

"Stay with her," Ashur instructed Daimon, his voice bearing tinges of worry. "I will return as swiftly as I can. We will form a plan to rescue Zadie."

Daimon nodded, his gaze never leaving Maj's face, as if by sheer will he could restore the strength sapped away.

"Come," Ashur said, turning to Nadine and Cricket, exhaustion lacing his words. "I will guide you."

He led them down the winding corridors of the pyramid, the walls adorned with intricate mosaics that shimmered with an otherworldly glow. They passed through archways draped with verdant vines, entering a room alive with exotic scents and the murmur of soft conversations. In the center lay a vast iridescent pool.

The tropical heat engulfed Nadine and Cricket as they entered, an extreme contrast to the dry heat of the in-between lands they had just left. The warmth was a welcome caress against their skin, a feeling Nadine was not accustomed to.

Barely clothed maidens glided with effortless grace through a maze of sterile-looking stations, each one housing a hybrid being, like the ones they had seen when first they walked through the pyramid. The faint light cast shadows on the creatures' exposed skin, highlighting the metallic chains that clung to their necks like brutal collars. It was evident that these poor creatures were undergoing some sort of experimentation. Their pained, lifeless expressions tugged at Nadine's heartstrings.

"Feels like a lifetime since we've been somewhere this wet," Cricket whispered. "Zadie . . ."

Nadine frowned. "I know. I don't want to leave her either."

Cricket nodded, a tear flowing down her cheek.

Ashur's hand hovered over the shimmering surface of the pool, his fingers weaving an intricate pattern in the air. With a flick of his wrist, the once placid waters began to swirl, spiraling into a vortex of magic that hummed with power. "Remember," he cautioned, his voice a grave rumble, "this passage is one way. Once you step through, there is no return."

Cricket's voice was full of panic. "I can't—I can't leave Zadie!"

Nadine's gaze fixed on the churning portal, her heart pounding like a war drum within her chest. She could feel the heat of resolve radiating off her skin, a fiery aura visible only to those who knew the true extent of her elemental nature. Every fiber of her being screamed for victory, for triumph. This would not be denied her.

"Cricket," Nadine said, her voice cracking as her eyes locked onto her sister's. "We have to move now. There isn't anything you can do for Zadie. But I—" The words caught in her throat. "I can't do this on my own. I need your help."

Cricket took a deep breath. "I don't want this." She nodded solemnly as she cast a lingering glance at the room they were leaving behind. "We should have left that stupid crown in that icy prison and figured another way to save Father and you." With a frown, she placed her hand in

Nadine's. "But you're the only one left," she huffed, "and all the paths have narrowed to here. Right now. Just you. And me. Here." Cricket sighed. "What choice do I have?"

Nadine firmly grabbed Cricket's shoulders, her lips pursed tightly. "You have a choice. When we get to summer court, you decide what you want for you. What you want for our family." Nadine began to tremble. "You decide. Do you hear me? You decide."

Cricket nodded her head vigorously. Without another word, Nadine tightly clasped Cricket's hand and confidently led her toward the portal. The sisters plunged into the swirling maelstrom together, the world around them dissolving into a blur of color and sound as they were whisked away from the tropical haven of the hybrids and maidens that lay hidden deep beneath the ocean.

As the rush of transition subsided, Nadine's mind teemed with the unknowns that lay ahead. They would emerge into the splendor and treachery of the summer court, a place where the air was thick with intrigue, and the scent of blossoms masked the odor of deceit. She couldn't imagine the state of chaos they might find, the alliances forged or shattered by Babs's unthinkable act.

CHAPTER 14
ZADIE

Sand. It invaded every crevice, every fold of Zadie's clothing, scraping against her skin with a coarse insistence that left her gasping for air. She fought to expel the gritty particles from her mouth, hacking and spitting out the sediment that clung stubbornly to her tongue and palate. The sand felt like an abrasive shroud, sticking to the sweat on her brow and the tears that clung to her lashes.

Her body was waging its own war against the venom that traversed through her veins—a poison gifted by the sting of the scorpion. A tingling numbness began at the site of the wound, spreading outward like tendrils of ice creeping over a sun-warmed rock. Confusion clouded her thoughts, each heartbeat thudding in her ears like the ominous drums of an approaching storm. The venom seemed to taunt her, whispering deceit to her senses, blurring the line between reality and hallucination.

Looking around, Zadie realized the full gravity of her situation. She was ensconced within the bowels of a scorpion's lair — the walls undulated with the movement of countless grains, shifting and whispering secrets in a language only the desert could understand. Stalactites of compacted sand hung precariously overhead, threatening to crumble at the slightest provocation. No doors or passageways offered hope of escape; the lair was a closed suffocating sphere, a trap designed by nature's cruel artistry.

In the midst of this sandy tomb, the creature that had brought her here paced with restless energy. He was a monstrous hybrid, his human head and arms grafted onto the arachnid body of a scorpion, a grotesque offspring of Tiamat's dark whims. His voice, though soft, carried the unmistakable cadence of chitin clicking against chitin — a sibilant symphony that was muffled within the claustrophobic space with unnerving clarity.

"Detestable Mer," he spat, his words dripping with venom to match the sting in his tail. "How dare you invade our realm, slay my kin, and think to steal what is ours?"

His pacing was a dance of fury, each step sending tremors through the sandy floor. With every pass, his segmented tail arched menacingly, a barbed lance governed by anger.

Zadie recoiled, curling her body tighter into a ball. She desperately wished to disappear, but it seemed impossible. His angry gaze pierced through her like hot daggers.

"Two of my siblings lie dead because of you and your kin!" he accused. "Ashur and Daimon, the traitors will pay!" His voice rose to a crescendo that seemed to make the very air vibrate with malice.

The scorpion man's agitation was palpable — a living thing that filled the lair with dread. Zadie knew she must tread carefully, for the beast before her was driven not only by hatred but by a need for vengeance. She held her breath, watching as he moved, knowing that any misstep could provoke a swift and deadly response.

Zadie shut her eyes, attempting to separate the effects of Babs's blood from the toxin of the scorpion. She felt sluggish from the bite, but deep down, she sensed a primal surge of energy unlike anything she had experienced before. What she couldn't find was herself. Was she still there underneath all of this? There was only one way to find out.

The air itself seemed to throb with the melody as Zadie's voice, soft and haunting, rose in a siren song. It was an old tune, one that spoke of the deep and endless embrace of the ocean, designed to soothe even the most savage beast into slumber. Yet the scorpion man was no ordinary creature. His eyes, human in shape but feral in their glare, narrowed as he perceived her intent.

"Enough!" he bellowed, his voice cutting through her enchanting lullaby like a knife through silk. With a speed that belied his size, he lunged forward, his pincers snapping viciously.

Zadie's reflexes saved her from a crushing grip, but not from being pinned beneath the colossal weight of his scorpion form. The stinger, with its jagged edges and needle-like tip, hovered menacingly just above her face. Its surface was slick and wet, coated in a fresh layer of deadly venom. The air around them seemed to crackle with tension as the creature prepared to strike. Every detail of the stinger was magnified, from the tiny droplets of venom to the pulsing veins that ran along its length. Her heart pounded in her chest as she braced herself for the inevitable attack.

The sting of fear was as potent as the threat of poison.

"Cease your pathetic attempts," he hissed, his humanoid mouth twisting cruelly. "You think to tame me with your petty tricks? I could prolong your pain, make you beg for mercy that will never come." His warning carried a promise of torment that made her blood run cold. "I am the least of my siblings' terrors. They would make you yearn for the kindness of oblivion."

She stilled, realizing the futility of struggle against her predicament. Her mind raced for another plan, anything that might offer a glimmer of hope. Why was her Mer song not working? Was it just in this place, or had she lost it permanently?

The lair was a trap of sand walls and shifting floors; there was no apparent escape, not for someone who couldn't melt into the grains as he did.

"What do you want from me?" she asked, her voice barely a whisper against the oppressive weight of her captor.

"You?" he scoffed, retracting his stinger but not his malice. "You are but bait, Mer. A lure to bring Daimon or Ashur back to this place so I may end them as they deserve and make their corpses a present to our great mother, Tiamat."

The revelation hit Zadie. It was not about her at all—she was merely a pawn in a much larger game of vengeance and hatred between siblings.

Zadie absorbed his words, each one a somber note in the symphony of her predicament. She realized that any chance of survival depended on her wits and her ability to outlast the twisted patience of a creature born of spite and nurtured by the dark will of Tiamat herself.

Her voice rippled through the stifling lair with a tremor of defiance that belied her dire circumstances. "You will be waiting forever. No one is coming for me," she confided, her eyes betraying her melancholy. "I thought Tiamat dead," she mused aloud.

The scorpion man chuckled, a sound as dry and grating as sand against stone. "Oh, sweet Mer," he said with scorn dripping from each word. "Do tell her that when you meet. She will find your ignorance quite amusing."

Zadie's heart pounded in her chest, the rhythm frantic as if trying to escape the reality of her situation.

He spoke out loud as his thoughts swirled and weaved like the intricate patterns on the sandy ground. "Once the barrier is breached again, Tiamat will break through and reunite this realm, the origin of all things, with the rest of the worlds. She will no longer be separated from the primordial waters and will reclaim authority over both land and sea. A new era will be birthed." His laughter echoed off the walls, a cacophony of madness and malice. "To think, all will bow before her, and you, Zadie, will be the catalyst for the glorious war that awaits. One era ends and another begins."

Zadie struggled to piece out the meaning of his words. They were trapped in a failed timeline, right? One that Atlantis guarded. One that Ashur was very reluctant to unseal—only agreed to open when he realized that balance between the worlds could only be obtained by returning the crown to whence it came.

It seemed irrational to believe that this place could be the origin of all things. It was so barren—lifeless. What could be the reason to cut the worlds off from the origin? What had happened to cause such a permanent separation? Zadie couldn't quite puzzle it out. However, whatever the reason, he clearly seemed determined to wage war. Whereas Zadie knew very little of war, she did know that truth rarely mattered when it came to starting one.

She hissed, her voice barely above a whisper, "I would rather die than play any part in your twisted fantasy."

She was exhausted, and a sense of hopelessness filled her. It seemed as though she would never experience happiness again. But that was ridiculous; of course she would find joy once more. She just needed to escape. She needed to return to Atlantis. But why? What was there for her? Her entire existence had been upended. So much loss.

"Death?" The scorpion man's pincers clicked together with consideration. "All in good time. I would be more than happy to grant you that kindness."

Before Zadie could react, his stinger arced through the air, swift and precise. Pain exploded in her shoulder, fierce and blinding, as the venom surged into her bloodstream. It was an inferno of agony, a searing heat that spread outward, engulfing her senses with its toxic embrace.

Her vision dimmed as her limbs grew heavy, her muscles betraying her with their sudden refusal to obey. The world tilted, and she felt herself slipping into darkness, a silent scream trapped within her paralyzed throat. The sensation was like being submerged in the abyssal depths, pressure mounting from all sides, squeezing the very life from her. And then, nothing but the dark.

CHAPTER 15
BABS

Babs could feel the crown atop her head buzzing with a vibrancy that matched the steady pulse of the ley line beneath her feet. The whispers of praise and power intertwined, creating a symphony that only she could hear, each voice vying for her attention. Draped in her emerald silk gown, she exuded the essence of summer's bountiful potential, embodying the princess persona that the realm had bestowed upon her as she settled onto her throne.

The space had welcomed her home when she had phased Liande, Gwylm, and herself into the summer court.

Babs's presence seemed to command the queen's hall itself, which now felt more intimate, as if reshaped by her newfound confidence. The vaulted ceiling arched like protective arms, the petroglyphs etched upon the walls no longer cryptic but narrating ancient tales that pulsed through her very being. Even the great waterfall appeared to greet her with its melodic cascade, a sound that once caused fear now a symphony of welcome.

Positioned beside her, Gwylm's close proximity was a silent support. The wolf's obsidian fur bristled slightly, his gaze fixed forward, mirroring the seriousness that under-pinned their purpose here. He was more than a compan-ion; he was an extension of her will, a shared sentience that grounded her amidst her new surge of power.

As her gaze drifted to her right, it landed on Liande. The regal figure perched firmly in the seat of the summer queen, her peach gown clinging to her form like morn-ing dew on a rose, revealing the sensuous landscape of her body. Memories of the night before flooded Babs's senses — the tactile pleasure of exploring Liande's supple flesh, the intoxication of her scent, the primal satisfaction of bringing her to the precipice of ecstasy. Her own body responded instinctively, an echo of desire that resonated from her core, hardening her nipples, awakening an ach-ing warmth between her thighs.

Babs ran her tongue over her sharp fangs, feeling them lengthen. It had been an exhilarating night of indulgence, satisfying both their primal cravings and merging their powerful magic. Babs savored the delicious scent of Liande that lingered on her skin.

Around them, the grandeur of the Queen's Hall was poised on the brink of monumental change. The golden statue behind them, and edifice to Sabina, once a towering emblem of supremacy, now seemed curiously dated, its lus-ter dimmed.

In this charged atmosphere, Babs sat with Liande, united in purpose. Together, they would usher in a new era — one that would see Sabella deposed and Liande claim the throne as their new queen.

Babs embraced this challenge, her senses sharpened by the crown's incessant whispers of power and rule.

The wraiths above them circled in a ghostly ballet, their presence a chilling caress against the skin, a visual testament to Liande's mastery over the ethereal for all to see and fear. Having tasted that power the evening before, Babs now understood why Liande had summoned them. The power of wielding the dead was like a thrilling forbidden pleasure, a grip that stung but brought immense satisfaction.

The expectant hush was shattered as the water in the grand pool roiled and surged. Babs's heart quickened. "Good, he comes," she murmured with a smirk. With a sound like the roar of winter winds, the winter king burst forth from the watery gateway, his entrance a spectacle of power.

He was followed by Ambrosias, the winter prince, whose very presence seemed to crystallize the air around him. In his hand, the prince held the returned crown, an artifact of chilling beauty. Their soldiers, a legion of fae warriors clad in silver armor that gleamed like the last rays of a dying sun over a field of snow, poured forth in their wake. Helmets obscured their faces, rendering them indistinguishable, save for their wings — blades of ice honed to lethal perfection.

Ambrosias, however, stood apart from his uniformed kin. His visage was unmasked, exposed for all to witness the glory and splendor etched into his features. But it was his wings that drew Babs's gaze, a living contrast to the frigid soldiers'. Vines, dark and supple, writhed behind him, a dance of nature's untamed spirit with barbs and berries adorning their lengths, a reminder of life amidst the wintry host.

The skies of the queen's chamber now teemed with these fae warriors, their presence a declaration of intent clear as the bright edge of a blade: They were here to witness Sabella dethroned and Liande elevated.

Babs glanced at Liande, whose eyes burned with ambition. Together, they would rewrite the tale of the summer
court, their fates entwined like the serpentine vines of Ambrosias's wings.

Sabella's regal form strode tall and commanding,
draped in a cloak of rich scarlet that seemed to engulf her
body with fiery intensity. Her eyes burned with wrath as
she entered the grand hall, where Liande sat arrogantly
upon Sabella's throne.

Babs couldn't help but smile at the sight of Sabella's
fury; it was only fitting that her downfall would be public
and excruciating. Today, Gran would finally have justice,
and Babs would be the instrument to bring it about. A Culebra would make things right.

As Sabella entered the room, her fiery anger filled every
inch of it, as intense as the blazing midsummer sun. The
summer fae trailed behind her, sensing her dark emotions
and shrinking away in fear. But soon, Liande and Babs
would end it all. Sabella's name would be erased from
memory by the time they were finished with her.

Next to her strode the imposing figure of Soren, the summer king. Despite his round and robust build, he moved
with a regal grace. He had been away on a long hunt for
many seasons, and this was Babs's first time seeing him in
the flesh. Of course, she had heard stories of his great valor
and kindness. Yet none had explained to her why he had
stayed away all this time, why he had neglected his duties
as king. But none could deny that Sabella clearly had not
missed the monarch and preferred to rule alone. Had she
somehow kept him from court?

Babs was taken aback as she watched all the male fae
from the summer court, who had accompanied the king on
the great hunt, flow into the throne room. Their dogs barked

fiercely as they caught sight of the unfamiliar winter trespassers. It was quite a contrast to the calm and composed wolves that were constant sentinels of the court.

The female warriors and priestesses appeared out of thin air, coming together in a perfect formation around the throne. The giant wolves stood by the sides of the warriors who were ready for battle with weapons in hand. No corner was left unguarded as summer fae materialized through walls, fully prepared for any threat.

"Interesting," Babs murmured under her breath, the crown atop her head buzzing with voices that echoed her thoughts.

Liande's light laughter cut through the cacophony of growls and wails. She leaned in close to Babs, her voice a velvet whisper that tickled the senses. "All the pieces are in place," she said, her gaze flickering with delight as she caressed Babs's hand. "Soren shall bear witness to the fall of Sabella, and from the ashes of her deceit, all minds will be made clear. My moment has come."

The wraiths above continued their haunting vigil, circling with an elegance that belied their mournful cries.

Babs glanced across the field of faces, each marked with the expectancy of the impending clash.

As Sabella surveyed the assemblage with a queen's confidence, a tumultuous silence fell upon the court. The winter king, a figure of frost and shadow, hovered above the simmering tension, his gaze locked with the fiery monarch.

"Why do you darken my hall uninvited?" Sabella's voice rippled through the chamber like heat lightning. "You are making quite a habit of it, aren't you, Warrin?"

Babs's eyebrow shot up in surprise, having never heard the winter king's name. Hushed whispers snaked through the court.

The winter king inclined his head slightly, his expression unreadable. "I come not to darken but to illuminate, Sabella." He smirked. With a deliberate gesture, he turned his attention to Liande.

"Your word, Lady, is the beacon that guides me," he said solemnly. "I am here to fulfill an oath." Answering the king's call, four guards descended from the sky with lightning speed and encircled Sabella, their swords drawn and ready.

A collective breath seemed to be held by all, the air charged with expectancy.

Sabella, ignoring the winter guards, watched the summer king as he left her side. She turned then to Babs. Her query cut through the stillness sharp as a scythe. "And who have you brought before us? Who dares sit upon my throne! Speak, Princess of Summer!"

Babs rose to her feet, shutting her eyes and feeling a surge of energy from the delicate crown resting atop her head. It filled her with confidence and strength, empowering her words as she spoke with a loud, resounding voice. "Though I was raised among the mortals, fate led me to your realm, where my humble goal was to find my rightful place. And it was Summer herself who chose me to be your princess, as witnessed by all during my crowning ceremony. As the foretold 'Balancer,' it is my duty to restore the balance that has been stolen from us by none other than our summer queen, Sabella." She stood before the two most powerful fae courts, ready to bring memory and equilibrium back to their realm.

Babs turned away from the crowd and faced the majestic golden statue of Sabella, towering high into the cavern's ceiling. The pulsing energy emanating from it was palpable. Babs closed her eyes and lifted her hands toward the heavens. With a focused mind and an incantation on her lips, she summoned rocks from the walls to crash into the massive statue, leaving deep indentations and reshaping its form. Worms wriggled out of the crevices and crawled up the statue, hungrily eating away at the edifice with fervor. As sand cascaded down to its base, the statue's form began to shift into that of Liande. The worms morphed into delicate butterflies and gracefully fluttered toward all of the enchanted fae in attendance, landing softly on each one and breaking the spell that had clouded their memories, causing them to forget. With renewed clarity, they were freed from Sabella's grip.

The anger of the queen of summer was unmistakable, her primal roar echoed throughout the cave.

Babs smirked. "Sabella, do you not recognize your own sister? The one you cursed and left forsaken in the mortal realm?" Her words were like sunlight piercing through fog, clear and revelatory. "Do you not remember Liande?"

An electric hush shrouded the court. The effect was instantaneous; memories surged forth, unfurling like ferns in the warmth of spring, as the spell of forgetting, once cast by Sabella's hand, crumbled away under the might of the Balancer's proclamation.

Sabella's face grew as pale as a waning moon as she witnessed the obliteration of her reign.

Audible gasps rippled through the crowd, a symphony of astonishment, as both winter and summer fae alike confronted the unveiled truth. The revelation hung in the air, palpable and transformative, altering the landscape of their reality with the simplicity of a single, powerful utterance.

The charged silence of the court fractured under the weight of a thousand reawakening minds, their collective amnesia dispelled by Babs's magic and declaration.

Within that tumultuous sea of consciousness, Babs sought and found a singular presence within the court, one that snagged her breath in a silent gasp of recognition. There he stood, the fae man whose reflection she had gazed from Liande's pool.

His eyes, deep pools of cerulean blue, locked onto hers with an intensity that felt like a physical touch, intimate and exposing. Sun-kissed hair fell about his shoulders in a careless cascade, framing a face that bore a smile both warm and enigmatic. The prince moved with an effortless grace, his lithe form adorned with a crown that was the twin of Babs's own.

In that moment, the air between them thrummed with unspoken promises and the allure of power that was seductive, gentle, yet undeniably kind. It was a power that called to Babs, whispering of a bond that transcended mere allegiance.

A sudden pressure against her leg broke the spell. Gwylm, ever the anchor in the storm, nudged her with his great black head, his eyes alight. Babs turned back to the unfolding drama before her.

"Liande," she murmured, the voices within her crown clamoring. The court remained still. "Justice for you. Justice for Nadine. Justice for Gran."

Liande stood, her body melding with Babs's. Their lips collided, in a feverish primal kiss. Babs's fangs delicately grazed Liande's bottom lip. She took a slow, tantalizing lick before gently biting her own tongue, letting their blood mix between them. A small trickle of crimson ran down their mouths.

"Justice for all, my dear princess," Liande whispered against Babs's mouth, her voice a velvet purr.

In a flourish of power that commanded the very air around them, Liande unfurled her wings—majestic appendages that shimmered with the kiss of winter's frost against the stunned backdrop of the court. Each beat of her wings caused the vines to writhe and dance. Babs had only witnessed one other pair like them—Ambrosias's.

With a grace that defied gravity, Liande ascended toward the vaulted ceiling, where the wraiths circled like heralds of the changing tide. "Today, you will bow before a deserving queen," her proclamation echoed.

Power thrummed within Babs, craving release upon she who had wronged her lineage.

CHAPTER 16
CRICKET

Cricket's delicate wings spread out, nearly healed, shimmering in the light of the fading portal. They were as translucent as gossamer, glowing with an otherworldly luminescence. Nadine gripped her hand tightly as they descended, their movements perfectly synchronized like a dance through the air. As they drew closer to the waterfall, the mist engulfed them, carrying them down to the heart of the summer court—a vast expanse of water that shimmered and sparkled with mysteries untold.

The surface of the water lay still, like a sheet of polished glass, perfectly mirroring the luminous cavern ceiling above. This eerie expanse was studded with fae warriors, their crystalline wings glistening like icicles in the dim light and producing an unsettling, tinkling noise as they hovered menacingly overhead. Their faces were hidden behind harsh, metallic helmets, but the tension rippling through their taut bodies was unmistakable. The hairs on Cricket's neck bristled in alarm.

Cricket's mind still struggled to grasp the horrifying reality of Sabella murdering Gran. It was a senseless, brutal act that defied all reason. Her hands trembled uncontrollably at the mere thought of Sabella's overwhelming power. Panic and regret churned within her, a storm of chaotic feelings. She should have acted, intervened somehow—done anything to prevent it. Instead, when Gran needed her most, she had been paralyzed by fear, unable to move. The weight of her inaction pressed heavily upon her chest, and shame painted her cheeks a deep crimson hue.

When she confronted the monstrous beasts in the failed timeline, she had steeled herself against the paralyzing grip of fear. Her sisters did not face the terrors alone. The struggle had exacted a toll—a price she found more bearable than the regret of inaction. One of the behemoths had actually crushed her—crushed her! She shivered at the mere recollection of its immense weight, the horrifying sensation of her bones splintering beneath it. The helplessness, the terrifying immobility—she cringed inwardly. She had never been afraid of animals before—not even serpents slithering through the grass. But now—now she dreaded that her newfound fear encompassed everything around her.

The air in the cavern was thick and still, as if every being within it held their breath. Winter soldiers flew tall and stoic, while summer fae glimmered like fireflies, guarding the perimeter of the pool. Every eye was fixed on the female fae who hovered in the air, high above the thrones, her presence commanding and powerful. The stillness among them was orchestrated, a shared pulse that connected them all.

Cricket's heart lurched in her chest as her gaze landed on the formidable Queen Sabella. The air around her seemed to ignite with a fierce, fiery aura, and Cricket couldn't help but shrink back in her presence.

Stepping around the winter guards that surrounded her, Queen Sabella strode toward her ornate throne. As she glided gracefully into her seat, the rich, crimson fabric of her gown cascaded behind her in a long train. She delicately adjusted the folds of the material, ensuring it fell just right against her body. The deep hue of the dress caught the light and seemed to glow with its own radiance, drawing Cricket's eye. "My throne. Mine alone," she spoke to the fae that soared above the dais.

The summer king joined her, ascending onto his own throne with a fluidity that spoke of timeless grace and regal poise. His crown was a mesmerizing symphony of golden vines, intricately woven and shimmering like captured sunlight. He was the very essence of nature itself, with skin as deep and rich as fertile earth and hair that cascaded in waves of molten gold.

His attire was notably casual, especially when contrasted with the opulent garb of the queen. He appeared as though he had just returned from a vigorous hunt, still carrying the rustic charm of the outdoors. Clad in soft, dark green riding britches and boots that seemed to meld with the forest's hues and a richly textured brocade overcoat that added a touch of elegance to his rugged appearance, he exuded an air of effortless elegance and merriment. The faint scent of leather and rose wafted from him, hinting at recent adventures through wild terrains. As he settled into his seat, the ground beneath him seemed to come alive, responding to his presence with an almost palpable energy. Vines burst forth from the floor, unfurling rapidly and snaking their way up the walls with an eager, almost fervent speed. Thorns and roses blossomed amidst the lush greenery, transforming the space into a vivid tapestry of life and color, creating a breathtaking backdrop for the court's solemn proceedings.

Cricket observed the summer king with a blend of curiosity and wariness, her eyes tracing every detail. Unlike the austere winter monarch, who floated above his men with an air of cold detachment and an aura of sharpness and steel, the summer king exuded a gentler strength. His form was robust, almost as if sculpted from the very essence of abundance. His eyes were deep, inviting pools of kindness, framed by a face that seemed to have been nurtured into existence by the fertile earth itself.

Yet, despite his serene exterior, a shadow of perplexity clouded his gaze. His eyes lingered on Queen Sabella, betraying an undercurrent of confusion that marred his otherwise placid expression.

Cricket's attention was captured by the magnetic intensity of Sabella's unwavering stare. Suspended above the eerily silent gathering, a breathtaking fae, draped in ethereal phantoms, held everyone's undivided attention. Horror wrapped its icy fingers around Cricket as a wave of recognition crashed over her. These were the spirits snatched from the graveyard on that fateful night when Bash had liberated Caroline from Rebecca's spectral grip. Cricket knew these souls! A surge of bile rose in her throat, revolted by the sight of these ghosts shackled like slaves to that mesmerizing fae. Had it been that beautiful fae that had given Bash the potion to give to Caroline? What could drive someone to enslave these spirits? To what end did she use them for her own selfish desires? Surely nothing was worth such cruelty toward these innocent beings.

"Look, Cricket," Nadine whispered, her voice barely more than a breath against the profound hush that cloaked the cavern. "There she is. There's Babs." Babs exuded a sense of royal poise as she stood before the ornate throne beside the queen.

Her stunning dress was a deep emerald, the fabric flowed gracefully around her figure, glimmering in the dim light of the throne room. Her posture was perfect, every move deliberate and commanding. Blood stained her plump lips. This majestic, rigid figure was unrecognizable as the sister she knew and loved.

Without uttering a single word or sparing even a fleeting backward glance, Nadine propelled herself forward, her fury etched unmistakably across her features. Whatever had driven Babs to steal the crown and abandon them all in the failed timeline, it was clear that Nadine was eager to make her answer for her deep betrayal.

The court's silence fractured as the regal fae aloft spoke with authority. "Your illusions are broken; the truth is exposed. I dare you to face me, Sabella!" Her declaration directed the winds of fate for them all. "If only you had left me alone. I was content as the princess of winter, but your paranoia and ruthlessness will result in your downfall, dear sister. I, Liande, will be your undoing." She floated lightly down to Sabella's side.

Cricket's breath hitched in her throat. It was at that moment that Ambrosias, the winter prince, descended toward the thrones with the force and presence of an unleashed tempest. His expression was as cold and unyielding as ice, betraying no emotion. Every muscle in his body was taut, radiating a palpable tension that chilled the very air around him.

With unnerving calm, Liande alighted before him, her gaze cutting through illusions unseen. "Is the glamor still upon you?" she murmured, reaching out to stroke his cheek, an intimate gesture. She pointed to his wings, the vines writhing in agitation with synchronization of her own. "You are my son. Deep in your heart, you must know."

Ambrosias stilled, his usual bravado faltering under the weight of her tender touch. Liande turned to seek the validation of the winter king, whose steely eyes held the truth of a history soon to be revealed.

Amidst the throng of fae, a hush fell as the winter king floated toward the thrones. His voice, though low, carried through the cavern with unwavering authority, echoing off the elegant arches and shimmering pool. "Let it be known," he began, "that Ambrosias is indeed a true son of winter." He paused, his verdant eyes resting on Liande. "Sired by me with Liande, not Sabella."

Cricket was swept up in a whirlwind of unraveling secrets, struggling with overwhelming emotions. Her heart was heavy for Ambrosias, who came from a world of royalty and power, far different from the humble treasures and simple pleasures of Baubles and Whatnots. He was entangled in a web of ambition and bloodlines, mysteries and sorrows, and familial betrayal.

A collective murmur rippled through the court, the air itself charged with the gravity of his pronouncement. Sabella's face remained a porcelain mask that betrayed no hint of the turmoil that surely roiled beneath. Liande's demeanor was the antithesis of her sister's — a portrait of vindication, her chest rising with triumph. She was no longer insignificant — no longer forgotten.

Cricket's eyes darted between them, wide with realization. Everyone saw it — sister against sister.

Ambrosias caught her gaze, and she could see the weight of the truth crushing him. The prince, who had been so sure and confident before, now seemed unsure and vulnerable. She was desperate to ease his pain.

"Let it also be known . . ." Liande's voice cut through the silence, each word a dagger aimed at the heart of deceit. "It is Sabella who has brought chaos to our kingdom. She snatched my crown, the symbol of winter's royalty, and hid it in a realm beyond our grasp. She ensnared me within a cursed form to rule over serpents and predators in the mortal realm."

Cricket's breath caught in her throat, a tempest of thoughts raging inside her mind. Babs, with her calm and unwavering demeanor, sat as if she were a statue carved from smooth marble—her eyes never leaving Liande. Beside her, Nadine leaned in close, whispering something urgent and intense into Babs's ear. The fury in Nadine's eyes stood in sharp contrast to the soft murmurs escaping her lips. Cricket longed to know what was being said between her two sisters.

"Furthermore," Liande continued, her eyes alight with fervor, "a spell of forgetfulness was cast upon all courts by Sabella's hand. She erased all memories of my existence and claimed my child as her own. Certain of Ambrosias's unwavering support, she had woven a tale that he was her own flesh and blood sired by the winter king, a fabricated familial bond that linked her to the icy dominion of the winter thrones. A spell that enchanted both kingdoms."

The surrounding fae whispered amongst themselves, the threads of history unraveling before their very eyes. Cricket watched as Ambrosias's world crumbled, his identity rewritten in the span of mere moments. Pain flittered across his features.

She could feel the shock radiating from him, a powerful and tangible force that resonated with her own soul. Her heart ached to reach out, to offer solace to the prince she was destined to join in both power and purpose. But her feet remained rooted.

"Look upon him," Liande implored, gesturing toward Ambrosias with a maternal fierceness. "See my son of winter, born of love and wronged by fire." She turned and glared at Sabella.

Ambrosias's frame trembled, caught in the vortex of revelation.

A hush settled over the cavernous expanse of the court as the winter king, his voice a chilling decree, bid his soldiers still themselves. "Winter bears witness to Sabella's treachery," he imposed, his eyes glinting with the frost of a thousand winters. "Summer's flame must do likewise." He turned to address the monarch beside Sabella's throne, whose presence was as lush and verdant as the untamed forest. The summer king nodded solemnly, acquiescing without words, his gesture commanding the silence and attention of his own court.

Cricket, her heart fluttering like the delicate wings at her back, felt the gravity of the moment suffocating the air. She watched as the two regal sisters faced each other, their fates entwined in a dance as old as the courts themselves.

The duel commenced with a whisper, a murmur of power that crescendoed into a roar. Sabella, cloaked in flames that danced like serpents around her form, unleashed torrents of fire toward her sister. Liande, rooted in the earth, countered with ferocity, summoning vines that surged forth to ensnare and quell the inferno.

The cavern became a tempest of elements clashing, the heat of summer's blaze grappling with the resilience of earthen might. Liande's magic shimmered with an emerald sheen, her connection to the land amplifying her strength, yet Sabella's flames were relentless, searing through defenses with wrath burning in her core.

As they fought, their magics painted the air with strokes of light and shadow, a violent tapestry woven from their fury. Sabella's next spell was a conflagration designed to consume, to leave naught but ash in its wake. The spell surged forward, a wave of destruction aimed at Liande's heart.

But Babs, the summer princess with hair like the twilight sky, intervened. With a cry torn from the depths of her soul, she leaped before Liande, her own crown ablaze with a protective aura. The life-giving fangs bared not in threat but in sacrifice, she absorbed the brunt of Sabella's wrath, a barrier between death and her ally.

"Enough!" Babs thundered. The very stones of the cavern seemed to tremble at the authority wielded by one so connected to the realm.

The battle paused, breath held collectively by the court as they beheld the defiance of a princess protecting her future queen. It was a stalemate painted in the violent hues of power and passion, a tableau that spoke volumes of the alliances and fractures within the family of fae.

Liande's high-pitched scream reverberated through the air as she threw her head back, her body thrumming with power. All color and life drained from her eyes. She raised her arms, commanding the spirits around her. With a low hum, they swarmed toward her, their iridescent forms swirling and dancing in a macabre display. The spirits' eerie green light swarmed Sabella, stripping away every drop of color and vitality until she floated before them as a ghostly apparition. Her once vibrant red dress faded into wispy mist, her hair turning thin and grey like smoke. Her once sensual flesh withered, dissolving into a translucent form as she completed her transformation into a listless spirit.

Babs's hand trembled as she reached out and grasped the golden crown that fell from Sabella's incorporeal form. Liande lifted her arms and began to chant in a low, melodic voice. The pool beneath them started to churn and swirl, forming a powerful vortex that seemed to pull at the very fabric of reality. Golden sparks danced on its surface, calling out to the spirits and drawing them closer. Cricket found it both exhilarating and terrifying to witness such raw power being wielded by Liande. As she witnessed the ruin of the fae who had taken her Gran from her, Cricket's tears of relief gushed freely.

With each passing moment, the vortex grew stronger, its pull becoming irresistible as the spirits quietly departed.

Liande heaved in deep breaths, her chest rising and falling rapidly. She gazed on with relief as the last of the ghosts vanished through the portal. All was now as it should be.

With a graceful hand, Babs lifted the gleaming crown for all to see. Its intricate details sparkled in the light, catching the attention of every onlooker. She then bestowed it upon Liande's head, her movements gentle and deliberate. Together, they ascended their thrones, basking in the weight of their newfound power and responsibility. The throne room was filled with a hushed reverence as all witnessed the coronation of the new ruler.

Cricket, her gaze locked on the unfolding drama, felt the whispers of her own destiny nudging against her consciousness. In the maelstrom of magic and emotion, she felt the call to rise and rule.

Ambrosias's eyes searched desperately through the throng until they landed on Cricket. With the grace of a winter storm, he swept down to her. The anguish of the past moments chiseled on his face held a beauty that was both soft and vulnerable.

"Cricket," he breathed, relief crashing into him like a wave. "I couldn't feel you — for days I couldn't feel you. The void was — intolerable."

She trembled, the silence between them heavy with unspoken thoughts. There was so much to share. Where should she start? "I was—" she murmured, playing with the hem of her Mer dress. "It's a long story."

He stretched out his hand, holding the winter princess's crown, which shimmered like frost beneath a moonlit sky. This artifact had cost Gran her life. The quest for it had altered her forever. This artifact had plunged them into the doomed timeline where Zadie still remained ensnared.

"Please," he implored, his voice a soothing balm, "you are meant for this. You were always meant for this."

The crown—a circlet of ice and promise— pulsed with ancient power. For a moment, Cricket hesitated. To wear it was to accept a life she'd resisted, to embrace a future steeped in duty and sacrifice. Gran's last request of her was not to do this. Not to join the winter court. Gran had always dreamed of a different path for her—of days spent amidst the curiosities of Baubles and Whatnots, not the intrigues of courts and crowns. But that life had crumbled to ashes along with the shop. Surely Gran would have changed her mind if she had known what was to come. Hadn't they all just witnessed the telling come true? All would agree the telling was about the Daughters of Inanna—Liande and Sabella.

"Liande, my mother, was the last bearer of the winter crown," whispered Ambrosias, his eyes reflecting a maelstrom of emotions. "Now it falls to you."

How could she deny him, in this moment. How could she deny herself what she felt was right in her heart.

She paused, pondering for one moment as Nadine's words came to her mind. The choice was hers. Not Gran's. Not Ambrosias's. Her choice. Hers alone.

She murmured, more to herself than to Ambrosias, "Nothing remains for me in the mortal world." If she stripped all away — all that everyone else wanted for her life, she knew this was what she wanted for herself. She wanted more. She wanted this. She looked into the deep pools of his eyes. She wanted him.

With a breath that felt like her first and last, Cricket bowed her head. Ambrosias, with hands that commanded the biting winds yet caressed her with the gentleness of falling snow, crowned her.

A powerful surge of magic, fierce and exultant, thundered through her very soul. It was a symphony of ancient princesses, their voices echoing in her mind, each one eager to share their wisdom from ages past. The warmth of their presence enfolded her like a roaring fire in the hearth on a cold winter's night, comforting and inviting her into their shared legacy.

Vasuki's serpentine voice echoed in her mind, overpowering all other thoughts. All Cricket could hear was a forceful demand to surrender. *"My strength, my control. You will bend and shed your autonomy, shed your desires. I will fill your speech, fill your throat."*

As Cricket closed her eyes, her hands trembled. She chanted ancient words and beckoned to the spirits of Culebra, their golden essence swirling around her body. Gradually, she began to levitate as their powerful energy merged with hers. Her physical form dissolved and transformed into a being of pure magic. She reveled in this new stature, knowing that she wielded unimaginable power. Addressing Vasuki, she declared, "I am in control now. You are but a humble servant to the crown and to me." With a flick of her hand, she commanded her to submit to her will.

As her feet gracefully touched the earth, Ambrosias materialized in front of her and gently kissed her hand.

"My beloved princess," he whispered with a twinkle in his eyes.

The cavern fell into a hushed silence, every fae within feeling the profound thrum of power resonating through the air in this singular, momentous occasion — the ascension of the new winter princess. All eyes were riveted on Cricket, whose delicate continence now shimmered with a rapturous light, like frost kissed by the morning sun, as the ancient legacy of winter powerfully settled upon her.

CHAPTER 17
ZADIE

Consciousness crept back to Zadie in cruel increments, the venom from the scorpion sting pulsating through her veins like molten fire. She lay motionless on the granular floor of the sandy lair, the dim glow of phosphorescent fungi casting eerie shadows on the walls. Her throat was parched, an arid desert swallowing her voice before it could beg for the water that her body screamed for.

Her vision wavered, the edges blurred as if she gazed through mottled glass, but panic anchored her to stillness. To move might draw attention; the scorpion monster's senses were surely as sharp as the sting that felled her. With each shallow breath, she prayed to remain unseen, a mere wraith in the creature's periphery.

A deep timbre rumbled through the chamber — a voice like thunder rolling over the distant horizon. It emanated from a figure she could not see, a silhouette shrouded in darkness so complete it seemed to absorb the feeble light around it. His words were a cryptic symphony, each syllable infused with the weight of untold eons.

"Mother Tiamat," he intoned, reverence lacing his speech, "primordial goddess of chaos, who reigned before the cosmos found order."

Zadie's mind raced. Tiamat—the name rang in her ears. She imagined the deity as a vortex of primordial forces, a maelstrom of creation and destruction from which all complexity had once sprung. Daimon and Ashur's mother.

"Time has forsaken us," the shadow continued, its voice a tempest contained. "Our great battle lost in the annals of eternity, we stand as remnants of the past, sealed from the march of time."

As the story unfolded, Zadie's heart thudded against her rib cage, a frantic drumbeat echoing the gravity of her predicament. Tiamat and her children—captives in chronological stasis while life surged forward beyond their reach. A prison made not of bars but of frozen, unyielding time.

She dared not stir, though every instinct cried out for action. Here she was, a Mer buried in sand, ensnared in the web of a forgotten war.

The scorpion man's words ebbed and flowed. "Storm Demon, we have a chance of escape and rule. Our time is now to right the wrongs of the past. We may yet be the victors." A resonant silence hung heavy in the air. Zadie realized that her journey was entwined with the fate of gods. Whether by chance or destiny, she was now part of this ancient tapestry, and only time—should it ever flow again—would unravel her role within it.

Zadie's throat, parched like the desert sands engulfing her, yearned for a single drop of solace in this arid prison. She lay still, eyes a mere slit, peering through the dimness at the towering figure of the scorpion man. His silhouette loomed, an embodiment of ancient power, his form both terrifying and awe-inspiring as he spoke with a voice that rumbled like thunder rolling over the deep.

The scorpion man spoke yet again. "Guardian of thresholds, keeper of sacred spaces, Storm Demon," he intoned, the timbre of his voice resonating with the weight of uncountable years spent in vigilant service. "I have captured the unworthy. My sting punished the trespasser. For Tiamat, Mother of Chaos, we endure and will overcome."

Zadie's heart quickened as she listened, a captive audience. The scorpion man was not merely a creature of legend; he was the staunch defender of Tiamat's realm, his every sinew wrought from devotion and duty.

"Through epochs I have watched," the scorpion man continued, the darkness itself seeming to listen. "The barrier stood unyielding, but my patience remained adamant as obsidian. My cunning will dawn the day that the seal fractures yet again, and from these depths, we shall emerge to rule."

From her vantage point, Zadie observed the subtle shift of shadows within the lair, the scorpion man's form an intricate tapestry of human intellect and primal instinct. He was guardian and warrior, a paradox melded into existence by a goddess's whim.

There were truths here, buried beneath layers of time and enigma, and she felt the inexorable draw to unravel them.

The scorpion man paused, his senses attuned to the subtlest vibrations. Zadie held her breath, the taste of fear metallic upon her tongue. He turned slowly, and though his eyes were pools of impenetrable night, she felt their gaze pierce her veil of invisibility.

"Water." Her voice was a raspy, cracked whisper, barely audible. Her lips were parched and swollen from lack of water, causing her speech to be strained and difficult. Every word that escaped her mouth was accompanied by a dry rasp, a reminder of the harsh conditions she had endured. The heat had beaten down on her relentlessly, sucking the moisture from her body until she could barely form words. She longed for even a drop of water to soothe her cracked lips and throat. She frantically searched her wrist, but her bracelet was missing. How long would she last in the unforgiving desert without her bracelet to draw water from the arid air and keep her hydrated? The thought brought a wave of panic crashing over her. She scanned the room for any sign of her bracelet, but all she could see was shadow and shifting sand. The dry, scratchy air filled her lungs as she desperately tried to push aside thoughts of dehydration and survival.

Zadie's consciousness flickered, teetering on the edge of the abyss as she lay curled in on herself. Her mind clawed its way back to alertness, her body protesting with every fiber of her being. The venom's influence lingered, an unwelcome guest clouding her senses.

She dared not move, her gaze locked onto the towering figure of the scorpion man. His silhouette was a dance of shadows and dread. Zadie's breath hitched.

The scorpion man's voice was low and gravelly as he recounted to the storm demon, "Ashur once stood upon the threshold and cast a glittering crown into our void. The act was shrouded in mystery, leaving all who witnessed perplexed and awestruck."

The storm demon countered, "Why did our treacherous brother offer such a prized possession to the forgotten realm?"

The scorpion man replied, "We knew not. But from that day, I kept a watchful eye on this entrance, my patience stretching as I waited for Ashur's return." The air around them felt charged, as if the very earth itself was holding its breath for what was to come. "It was during one of those vigil nights that I glimpsed Daimon, the fae of the sea, with others weaving through the forgotten realm." He waved his hand in the direction of Zadie. "My instinct had surged, recognizing the treacherous Son of Tiamat. I kept to the shadows and watched—discerning an opportunity to snatch within my grasp. And when chance presented itself, I dragged this Mer from their midst, bringing her here."

The storm demon questioned, "Do you believe her to be the key—the Mer whose destiny might unlock our shared prison?"

As Zadie's vision swam into focus, she observed the fusion within her captors: the calculated intelligence that plotted behind ancient eyes and the primal force that could rend the very sand around them. They were creatures of intellect and instinct. One exterior armored and the other cloaked in shadow. Yet within them both dwelled a cunning that belied their monstrous forms. Sentinels born of the earliest chaos, embodying the ferocity and wisdom necessary to protect the sacred, to examine the gateway that held back the tide of Tiamat's legacy.

"Water," she whispered again, her voice no more than a sigh lost in the claustrophobic cavern. Despite the weakness that threatened to claim her, Zadie's spirit refused to succumb to despair.

The sand beneath Zadie shifted imperceptibly as she lay in the dimly lit lair, her senses dulled by venom but her mind desperately clinging to consciousness. Across the small chamber, where shadows clung to shifting sand, the two figures loomed large and ominous. Beside the scorpion man, the storm demon's form swirled with tempestuous energy, its voice thunderous even in hushed tones.

"Tell me, why did you not bring this information directly to Tiamat?" The storm demon's question reverberated like distant lightning, casting a palpable tension throughout the space.

"Patience," the scorpion man rumbled, the timbre of his voice resonant with authority. "We must first consult the recorder of destinies. Our mother, Tiamat, values the order within the chaos she commands. To reveal the presence of the Mer without understanding her woven fate would be folly."

"Indeed," the storm demon acquiesced, its form contracting. "The recorder of destinies, keeper of the ledger that binds mortal deeds to their eternal threads. A wise counsel to seek before we proceed."

Zadie strained to focus, her vision blurring at the edges as she absorbed their conversation. She knew of the recorder of destinies—a being said to possess knowledge of every soul's path, their past and future eternally inscribed upon ethereal scrolls. That such entities were more than mere legend stirred both awe and fear within her.

"Her fate could illuminate our path," the scorpion man continued, his words measured and deliberate. "Should the recorder decree that this Mer has a role in the liberation of our kin, then surely Tiamat would see the prudence of our discretion."

"And if not?" The storm demon's inquiry held an edge sharper than any blade.

"Then we shall deal with the Mer accordingly. But let us not act in haste. Our plan must be flawless if we are to succeed in freeing ourselves from this temporal prison, to once again reign in unbridled chaos of creation."

Zadie's heart hammered against her rib cage. Her fate, it seemed, was to be decided by forces beyond her comprehension, arbiters of destiny who held the power to either aid or obliterate her existence.

As the two sentinels of Tiamat's realm turned away, their forms melding with the darkness, Zadie remained motionless, a silent observer. Her anger churned in the depths of her stomach.

Her vision swam, edges blurring into the dimness.

"Water," Zadie rasped, her voice cracking the silence.

The two guardians turned toward her, eyes meeting her form with a mixture of curiosity and caution. The scorpion man's gaze held a sharpness, assessing, calculating.

"Your name," the storm demon demanded, his tone a rolling thunder.

"Zadie," she answered, defiance fueling her strength. "I am of the Culebra line, fae of the sea."

For a moment, the chamber stood still.

"Take me to the recorder of destinies if you must." Her demand cut through the tension. "But first, water."

"Very well, Mer," the scorpion man conceded, his movements deliberate as he retrieved a vessel of water from the shadows.

Zadie accepted the offering, the cool liquid a balm to her parched throat. She would live.

"Lead me to my fate," she insisted, her voice no longer a whisper.

In the eyes of her adversaries, there flickered a grudging respect—a recognition that even bound by circumstance, this daughter of chaos and order would not surrender without asserting her right to shape the narrative of her own existence. Or at least hear it.

CHAPTER 18
NADINE

The coronation had ended, the summer court's grandeur bathed in a golden hue as the last of the daylight caressed Babs's throne. Nadine stood at the periphery, an observer in her own lineage's pageantry. Her gaze flitted from Cricket's radiant smile to Babs's regal poise.

A solitary tear betrayed Nadine's stoic facade, trailing down her cheek like molten silver. It was not jealousy that pricked her heart but a longing for a life unclaimed, for the warmth of a mother's embrace. The sound of a father's laugh. These were treasures she had been denied, her existence a mere shadow within the cold walls of the winter court.

"Never," she whispered, her voice barely audible as her hand tenderly caressed her belly. The life within her stirred. "The courts will never know you," she vowed, her will hardening like ice. "I will shield you from this madness."

As if on cue, the winter king rose in midair, his presence demanding. With an elegance that defied his formidable frame, he inclined his head to the summer king. "By your leave, we depart in peace."

With gentle acknowledgment, the summer king murmured incantations that danced on the edge of hearing. A ripple disturbed the once-placid waters of the pool at the heart of the room, growing into a tempestuous whirlpool that spiraled upward in a column of iridescence. Spectral lights flickered, casting phantasms upon the faces of all who watched.

The winter fae, wings spread wide, were caught up in the spell's embrace. They swirled through the air, their bodies suspended in the vortex before descending gracefully into the portal. Nadine felt the pull of the magic, an order to cross realms that was both thrilling and terrifying.

As they emerged on the other side, the chill of the winter lands embraced them, the mirror of ice reflecting the haunting beauty of their destination. The ice castle was a dazzling sight to behold, its walls adorned with elaborate artwork, each piece a masterpiece that paid tribute to the majestic power of winter. Ice gargoyles stood guard solemnly, their eyes fixed on the guests below. The detailed scrollwork, carved from ice and snow, climbed up the vaulted ceilings like delicate lace crafted by celestial hands. The ribbed arches resembled an exposed exoskeleton, leading up to a magnificent oculus where snowflakes gently drifted down upon them all. They occupied a world of perpetual snow.

Nadine lingered, her eyes fixed on the imposing glass that now separated worlds. She shivered, not from cold but from the darkness that seemed to emanate from its depths. Her fingertips traced the jagged fissure that marred its surface, pondering the force required to fracture such a powerful enchantment.

"Such a curious thing, aren't you?" she addressed the mirror directly. "What secrets do you hide behind your reflective veneer?" she murmured, more to herself than anyone else.

The echo of her own voice served as a reminder of the isolation that cloaked her despite the throng of courtiers that rushed about readying the hall for the evening's merriment.

All retired to don their finest for the celebration that was to ensue. Cricket had been whisked away leaving her alone to get dressed and ready for the evening. She quickly bathed in warm water, the sensation of it refreshing her tired body. She dried off with a soft towel and slipped into a long flowing silk gown, its vibrant color and delicate fabric complementing her features. The gown flowed gracefully down to her feet, draping over her soft slippered toes as she hurried back to the main hall.

As the festivities commenced around her, Nadine's thoughts turned inward. She would secure a future for her child, one far removed from the splintered reflections and broken promises of these realms.

Her gaze swept over the roaring fires in the many fireplaces lining the vast hall. They crackled defiantly against the encroaching cold, their flames dancing across the army of long wooden tables groaning beneath the weight of savory feasts.

As she approached a towering window, its panes stretched high and wide, framing a vista that she knew by heart.

The castle, with its intricate flying buttresses, dug its fingers into the rugged mountainside, which was blanketed in a perpetual layer of glistening snow. The dark forests below were serenely dusted in white, like a peaceful dream. Above, the setting sun painted the sky in hues of dwindling flame, while dark clouds meandered beneath them like somber nomads on their journey. Nadine exhaled, her breath fogging the glass.

The solemn sound of steel gracing marble drew her attention back to the throne room. The winter king, his regal presence commanding silence among the courtiers, knelt before the snow queen.

The snow queen's regal figure commanded the attention of all who laid eyes upon her. Her elegant form was a stunning display of ethereal purity, draped in a floor-length white gown adorned with delicate layers of silk and shimmering with tiny pearls and diamonds. The puff sleeves added an air of grandeur, while her white fur cape cocooned her like a protective shield against the winter chill. Yet it was her crown that dazzled the eye with its countless diamonds, scattering rainbows in every direction. One could not help but feel compelled to kneel before her in silent reverence.

Her hair cascaded down her back in a waterfall of pure white, reminiscent of doves taking flight. The only hint of color on her otherwise pale figure was the delicate pink hue of her full lips. Around her neck hung a massive necklace made of shards of glass, each one reflecting the light with dazzling clarity. But upon closer inspection, tiny droplets of blood could be seen trickling down her porcelain skin, staining her cleavage and bodice in an ombre effect from deep crimson to pristine white. These were the marks of her power, a visual reminder of how she maintained her reign over this winter kingdom.

With reverence befitting his devotion, the king kissed her hand, the tenderness of the act juxtaposed with the formidable power he wielded.

"Behold our snow queen," he proclaimed, his voice resonating with pride.

Above her head, bees hovered lazily, their translucent wings catching the light in a ghostly shimmer. The court maintained a respectful distance, bowing their heads in veneration. Nadine watched, feeling an unexpected kinship with these creatures who thrived in the chill of her elemental opposite. She stood apart, her fire essence concealed yet burning brighter with the life growing within her—a secret ember waiting to ignite.

"May her reign be as eternal as winter itself," someone called out nearby.

"May it be so," Nadine echoed quietly along with all in the room, the words tasting like ash upon her tongue. The court's merriment could not reach her, for her thoughts were ensnared by the reality of her plight.

Nadine watched on as Ambrosias escorted Cricket through the throng of onlookers. Her sister had changed into an elegant sky-blue ballgown made of shimmering silk. The off-the-shoulder sleeves streamed behind her as she walked, accentuating her slim waistline.

Her wrists and neck sparkled with strands of blue sapphires, while diamonds were intricately woven into her hair. Each step she took exuded grace and confidence, as if she had always been destined to be a princess. Their crowns, ornate with the intricate filigree of the winter court, shimmered with a light that mirrored the icy grandeur surrounding them. The prince's firm grip on her arm looked to be both a comfort and a chain, guiding Cricket toward the throne where the snow queen awaited, her gaze acute and expectant.

The queen's fingers—long, slender, tipped with long nails as blue as the heart of an iceberg—cradled Cricket's face with surprising gentleness. Her scrutiny was thorough, leaving trails of cold fire on the young princess's skin. A pair of kisses, lighter than a snowflake's touch, graced Cricket's cheeks before the queen withdrew a ring from her own finger. Holding it aloft, she declared in a voice that resonated like ice chimes, "A shard of our very portal, a symbol of unyielding loyalty to our realm. May you wear this always, Princess, as a testament to your fidelity."

As Cricket slid the ring onto her finger, a transformation subtle yet profound overcame her—the hue of her eyes shifting into a chilling reflection of the snow queen's own salient blue. Nadine watched from the periphery.

"Let us feast!" boomed the king, his proclamation echoing off the frozen walls. Violins sang and drums throbbed as servants unveiled platters piled high with exotic fare. The court indulged, laughter mingling with the harmonies of the music, but Nadine's appetite lay forgotten upon her plate.

She observed Ambrosias draw Cricket close, his lips grazing her ear, igniting a blush upon her cheeks. But their whispered intimacy quickly soured, replaced by creased brows and urgent tones. Nadine edged nearer, straining to catch their words masked by the cacophony of celebration.

"I must return for Zadie," Cricket insisted, her voice threaded with anxiety. "I can't abandon my sister to that desert of death!"

"Believe me, dearest, I yearn to aid you," Ambrosias replied, frustration sharpening his usually smooth tone. "But paths between realms are sealed; it's beyond my reach."

"Yet we traversed such a path to arrive here from summer," Cricket countered, her logic as irrefutable as it was desperate. "Surely another exists—one that leads to my sister."

Nadine, unable to hold her silence any longer, interjected with a voice laced with quiet urgency. "I believe Ambrosias has promised you happiness, yes? I am sure he will find a way." Nadine tilted her head down and gazed up at Ambrosias with a demure smile.

Ambrosias ran a hand through his silver locks, betraying his inner turmoil. With a shake of his head, he turned away, leaving a trail of frosty air in his wake. Nadine watched him go. She would find a path for Cricket, for Zadie, for all of them.

Nadine's gaze lingered on the retreating figure of Ambrosias, his broad shoulders a testament to the burdens he bore as prince. She did not envy him. Yet it was Cricket who now occupied her thoughts, her sister adorned in the regalia of royalty but ensnared by its gilded chains. With a discreet nod, Nadine beckoned her sister away from the thrumming heart of the feast to a shadow-draped alcove where confidences could be guarded from prying eyes.

"Cricket," Nadine began, her voice a whisper of urgency amidst the din of celebration, "you wield newfound power with your station. Use it—free our father and me. Send us back home to Mama. Once there, I will find a way back to the city under the water and help free Zadie."

"Zadie remains my main priority," Cricket replied, her tone resolute yet laced with concern. "Ambrosias has ensured our father's comfort; he's now esteemed within these walls. And you, dear sister, shall stand as high lady to the winter princess."

"High lady?" Nadine echoed, the title hollow. "I am to stay at court, then?"

"Indeed," affirmed Cricket, her gaze steady. "Honestly, I feel like I have fallen into one of my favorite books. Look at this dress!" She twirled around slowly, taking in the way the silk fabric gracefully draped over her body. "I have several closets full of them, all gifts from the queen herself. Oh, and the jewelry, the jewelry!" Cricket clapped her hands like a tiny child.

Nadine grabbed her hand and looked at the shards of glass that were the ring she proudly wore as a gift from the queen. "Doesn't that hurt? The way it's digging into your skin?"

Cricket's eyebrows rose. "Whatever are you talking about?"

Blood trickled down Cricket's finger, puddling in the crevice of her nail bed. "You are bleeding. Doesn't that hurt?"

"I'm not bleeding. Whatever are you going on about?"

"How can you say that? The shard from the mirror that you are wearing on your finger is biting into you and causing you to bleed. Just like the queen's necklace. Surely you see the blood dripping down her neck."

Cricket scanned the vast hall. "You are speaking utter nonsense. The queen is not bleeding, nor am I." She turned rapidly and grabbed both of Nadine's hands. "You must help me discern friend from foe. When I am well acclimated, you can go home to Mama."

"Time is a luxury I do not have," Nadine countered, her fingers digging into Cricket's soft flesh. "Please, release me from this court's madness," begged Nadine, her plea wrapping around them like the tendrils of a vine seeking sanctuary.

Cricket parted her lips to respond, but the moment fractured as the king appeared at her side. With an imperious gesture, he ushered Cricket toward the dais where the snow queen awaited, the throne beside her vacant and expectant.

Nadine stood alone once more, her eyes tracing the easy camaraderie between Cricket and the snow queen, their laughter mingling with the crackle of fires. She was alarmed that Cricket was unaware of the magic that pierced her. Beside the king, Ambrosias's jest elicited a rumble of mirth, his features momentarily unguarded.

"A hunt," the king proclaimed, his voice resonating with eagerness. "Yes, Ambrosias, a splendid notion. The wilds call to us."

Nadine lingered in the shadow of a grand, ice-sculpted pillar, her gaze sweeping across the throng of revelers. The feast before her unfolded like a tapestry woven with mirth and opulence, the air alive with the clinking of goblets and the whispers of silk. Laughter rippled through the court, a cascade of joy that seemed to mock her solitude.

Each chuckle that rose from the assembly tightened the knot in her throat, the weight of isolation pressing upon her chest with an almost tangible force. As she observed Cricket, now ensconced amid royalty, Nadine's fingers brushed against the slight swell of her stomach, the secret life within her stirring like the faintest wisp of flame.

She swallowed hard, the effort scraping raw against her dry throat. The irony was as cruel as winter's bite; here she stood, surrounded by kin and courtiers, yet the chasm of disconnect could not have been more profound. Her mission, the very purpose that had once ignited her spirit like the fiercest blaze, now lay in ashes at her feet. She was alone.

Nadine felt the sting of tears threatening to breach their barriers. She blinked them back fiercely, refusing to grant them passage. No, she would not let the court witness her despair. They would not see her falter.

Alone.

Alone.

Alone.

She hurried out of the grand hall and onto a sweeping balcony. She gulped the biting air as if she were drowning. She gripped onto the icy railing, focusing on the pain inside her chest. And she looked down.

CHAPTER 19

BABS

The throne room of the summer court shimmered with the verdant glow of eternal June, its walls alive with the rustle of leaves and the soft murmur of blooming life. Liande and Babs, entwined by their common triumph and shared authority, sat regally upon thrones transformed from hard stone to soothing ancient oak as Soren, the summer king, transformed the landscape. Their crowns, a manifestation of their triumph, glinted as if capturing the very essence of sunlight.

Babs's, hair cascaded like a waterfall over her throne's back, as she tilted her head to regard the newly crowned summer queen beside her. "Where did you send Sabella and all the souls?" she asked, curiosity overtaking her.

"Back to the mortal realm whence I found them. Sabella is doomed to roam the human plane as a wraith," Liande responded. "My gift to you." The vengeful fire that had propelled Liande to dethrone her sister had cooled into smoldering embers. "Your sister Cricket need not harbor you ill will. The balance has been restored, in full." Liande reached out and grasped Babs's hand tenderly.

"Restored," Babs echoed thoughtfully, feeling the whispers of her predecessors stir within her crown, their voices a constant cacophony at the edge of her consciousness. She wondered, not for the first time, where she ended and the crown began. For that matter, where did Liande end and Babs begin? Her loyalty to Liande—a fusion of lust for power and the raw magnetism between them—was a dangerous dance. One that she had surrendered to fully.

Soren, the summer king whose majestic bearing complemented his queen, rose from his seat with the grace of a lord assured of his welcome. A ripple of suspense cascaded through the assembled fae, each one attuned to the subtle shifts of power that constantly ebbed and flowed around them.

"Let us speak now of peace," Soren proclaimed, his voice resonating with an undercurrent of strength. "Our realm now thrives, untouched by the shadows of discord thanks to the braveness of our queen and princess. We enter a time of merriment, of reaping the harvest so diligently nurtured." His gaze slid toward Liande, laden with the heat of the approaching solstice.

Liande, who had tasted the bitterness of betrayal and savored the sweetness of revenge, inclined her head. She acknowledged both the declaration and the depth of intent behind the king's proclamation. Her lips curved into a smile that held the secrets of midnight rendezvous and whispered intrigues.

Babs observed the exchange, noting the currents of desire weaving through the political tapestry before her. She understood the utility of such alliances; her own path was paved with similar machinations. Her eyes followed the summer prince as he navigated his way through the crowds, stopping to chat and spread cheer.

Beneath the surface of Babs's poised exterior, a tremor of genuine emotion flickered. And as the prince extended his hand to a young soldier, she wondered what the foundation of their alliance, if there was to be one, would be. Surely they would get to know one another.

With Liande it had been easy. They both wanted power. They both wanted revenge. Babs had found Liande's ways intoxicating, mesmerizing. Today had culminated into a satisfaction she could have never attained on her own. But there was a bitter aftertaste in her mouth. At some point she would have to face her sisters. Face Mama.

With a gentle touch, the prince petted the young soldier's dog. His hand was delicate and soft, like a butterfly's wing. As she looked at the exchange, she saw nothing but warmth and tenderness. But what secrets lay within the depths of his heart?

The thrum of music rippled through the air, weaving its way between the revelers and the laden tables that groaned under the weight of summer's bounty. Wine poured like liquid rubies, shimmering in crystal goblets while laughter, bright and unrestrained, cascaded through the court of the summer realm. Courtiers, priestesses, healers and warriors, resplendent in their finery, moved like painted figures in a living tapestry—a testament to the prosperity and joy that Soren had so confidently proclaimed. The court was whole again.

Babs stood at the edge of this merriment. She was the earth embodied, the strength of her lineage pulsing beneath her skin—a Culebra princess cloaked in the regalia of the summer court. The whispers of her predecessors entwined with the will of her crown. She breathed this new reality in.

It was then that the prince approached, his lithe figure and ethereal grace clinging to his movements. His eyes found hers across the distance, and Babs felt the inexplicable pull, an invisible thread woven by fate or perhaps by the whispered desires of her own heart.

"Princess," he said, his voice a melody unto itself, "you have graced my dreams more often than the stars have kissed the night sky." A bold declaration, yet it carried the softness of sincerity that made her falter.

"My prince," she replied, her voice betraying none of the shyness that suddenly clenched at her throat. "To dance in dreams is one thing, but to tread upon the air with you here . . ." Her words trailed into silence as he extended his hand, an invitation she could not—would not—refuse.

His fingers closed around hers, and they stepped into the dance, moving amidst the other courtiers with harmonious precision. A smile tugged at the corner of his mouth, "Let there be no boundaries between us. Call me by my name. Call me Felix." Then, as if the very music commanded it, they ascended, spiraling upward until they soared beneath the vaulted ceiling of the great hall, carried by his great wings, vines of ivy and rose. Below them, the court became a jeweled kaleidoscope, a whirl of colors and light that dazzled the senses.

"I once saw your reflection in Liande's pool," Babs confessed, breathless with the magic of flight and the proximity of the prince who had unknowingly haunted her thoughts. "Even then, I felt . . . a connection."

He spun her, holding her tight, his wings keeping them adrift. The world tilted delightfully as her laughter mingled with his. How good it felt to truly laugh again.

His smile was warm. He parted his lips and said, "Then perhaps our destinies are as entwined as the vines that embrace the ancient oak," he mused, gazing down into her wide brown eyes.

As they danced above the revelry, the court looked on, admiration shining in their eyes. In this moment, Babs was more than a princess of summer; she was a vision of hope, of beginnings that bloomed under the sun's tender caress. And though she had always worn a mantle of confidence, there, in the skies with Felix, she revealed a tenderness that none had ever glimpsed.

The crown upon her head, usually so insistent with its demands, seemed to quiet, allowing her this reprieve — a chance to feel not just the earth beneath her feet but the sky within her grasp. And in that boundless expanse, she found a sense of lightness that had eluded her for so long.

The song eventually drew to a close, and Felix guided her descent, their feet touching the ground once more amidst the applause of their peers. The warmth of belonging swelled within her, and Babs knew that, for all her ambition and the whispers of power that threaded through her every thought, happiness might just have found a place within her after all. They took their seats at the front of the hall.

The vibrant notes of a lute entwined with the lilting melody of flutes, beckoning even the shyest of fae to the dance floor. As the song swelled, Liande, in her splendor as the newly crowned summer queen, took Soren's hand. Their bodies moved in harmony, an echo of their reign, fluid and sure. The king's gaze upon Liande was one filled with merriment, his movements a gallant vow to match her step for step in both dance and rulership.

Babs watched from her throne, her heart thrumming in time with the music. It was a sight to behold — their leaders joining as one with the rhythm, setting the cadence for all others to follow. The court responded in kind, a flurry of synchrony, as though each member shared a single heart-beat. Every twirl and leap was a testament to the peace that now mantled the realm, a tangible sense of joy that perme-ated the very air they breathed.

As the last chord lingered, Felix, seated next to her, a prince of summer's grace, lifted her hand to his lips. The brush of his kiss sent ripples through the air, a silent ac-knowledgment of the transformation she'd undergone. No longer vengeful. No longer angry.

"I see happiness in your eyes," Felix murmured, his voice a low thrum that only she could hear over the din of celebration. He shifted his weight to draw closer to her.

It was an observation that pierced the veil of Babs's usual stoicism, striking a chord within her — a recognition of the change that had taken root deep in her soul. She met his gaze, and for a moment, there was nothing else — no courts to impress, no power plays to consider — just the truth of his words reflecting back at her. She was happy — truly happy.

Babs's chest swelled as she fought the urge to let her emotions cascade in shimmering teardrops. The crown upon her head, a circlet woven from summer's breath and earth's embrace, hummed with the jubilant echoes of her predecessors, their whispers now dulcet tones of approval that melded with her own burgeoning sense of belonging.

The joy and celebration washed over the court in a daz-zling display of colors and lights, heralding a new era of unity and revelry. Sitting on her throne, Babs felt a sense of joy that kept her grounded amidst the whirlwind of fes-tivities. The air was filled with a lightness that matched the merriment all around her, bringing a palpable sense of to-getherness to the atmosphere.

She drew in a steady breath, the rich, loamy scent grounding her. Her eyes, usually so adept at surveying any terrain for advantage or threat, now softened as they took in the sight of her people. She could command the very soil beneath their feet, sway the creatures that roamed the forests to her will, but it was this moment — this culmination of trials and triumph — that commanded her.

A murmur of admiration threaded through the crowd, and though Babs was accustomed to leading, to being the fulcrum around which her sisters orbited, nothing had prepared her for the warmth that now suffused her being. It was more than acceptance; it was a homecoming.

"Princess," a voice called out, a resonant timbre that carried over the harmonies of celebration.

She glanced over at Felix, the prince whose dreams had intertwined with hers long before either had set eyes upon the other.

"Your radiance outshines even the stars tonight," he praised.

Babs allowed herself a small smile, one that rarely graced her lips — a smile not born of strategy or bravado but of genuine contentment.

Her heart now trembled with vulnerability. The summer princess, the Culebra of earth and commander of nature's bounty, felt an unfamiliar tremor within her — a flutter of hope that perhaps, amid the grandeur and the politics, there was space for her own happiness.

"Thank you, Felix," she said, her voice barely above a whisper, lest she shatter the fragile beauty of the moment. "You can call me Babs."

And as she held back tears, Babs knew, with a certainty that rooted itself deep into the marrow of her bones, she was finally home.

CHAPTER 20
ZADIE

The world above was a furnace, but beneath the sands, where Zadie clung to the ridge of the scorpion man's back, it was an inferno. Grit bit into her skin as they tunneled upward, a storm of heated granules whipping around them. She squinted against the stinging onslaught, sweat trickling down her forehead and mixing with the grains to form a muddy paste on her cheeks.

"Are you sure we shouldn't take her directly to Tiamat?" The storm demon's voice resonated through the shifting dunes, his form a swirling vortex of dark sand that flanked their hasty escape.

"I am resolved," replied the scorpion man, his voice a soft, sibilant whisper that somehow cut through the howl of displaced terrain. "We proceed to the recorder of destinies. My way."

Once they emerged from the scorpion man's lair, the relentless sun scorched down upon them, the desert stretching endless and barren before their eyes. The air shimmered with the heat, making the horizon dance like a mirage.

As they skirted the edge of a river long surrendered to the arid clutches of the land, Zadie observed the tenacity of life in this desolate place—tiny lizards skittering across hot stones, insects burrowing into whatever moisture the earth still cradled in its deep crevices.

"Look at them," she murmured, the words almost lost in the vastness around her. "Surviving in a world so devoid . . . I can't imagine a life without the embrace of the great oceans."

Zadie's gaze lingered on the undulating patterns left by a snake, a brief narrative of existence etched into the ephemeral canvas beneath her. Here, in the domain of earth and air, every moment seemed a struggle, every breath a conquest over the unyielding thirst of the desert.

"Your oceans have their own trials, Mer," the scorpion man intoned, noticing her distant expression. "But here, survival is an art perfected by few."

"An art indeed," Zadie agreed, turning her attention back to their path. She needed to learn that art, and fast.

Together, they traveled onward, the scorpion man's clawed legs leaving deep impressions in the sand, the storm demon trailing behind like an omen of tempests yet to come. Zadie's mind swam with thoughts of destiny and fate, the weight of her journey growing heavier with each step toward the enigmatic presence of the recorder.

The desert stretched before them, an endless canvas of gold and heat. Zadie clung to the scorpion man's broad back, her fingers digging into his carapace as he navigated the dunes with a grace that belied his monstrous form. The particles of sand clung to her skin, an abrasive mantle that chafed with every jostling movement.

"Tell me," Zadie began, her voice barely audible over the whistle of the wind, "about the Great War — the one that sealed you here with Tiamat."

The scorpion man's stride faltered. He seemed to weigh her request, his mandibles clicking softly.

"Long ago, before the sands devoured time itself, there was a conflict between gods so severe it shattered realities," he started, his tone somber, reflecting the gravity of ancient grievances. "As the mother of all hovered above the chaos, Tiamat's essence swirled and coalesced into powerful beings — the gods. They emerged from her chaotic energy with force and noise, causing turmoil and conflict among themselves. As their competition for dominance intensified, their battles threatened to destroy everything in existence."

As she listened to the story, Zadie's fingers curled into the coarse texture of the scorpion man's carapace. She could feel the roughness against her skin, a reminder that she was still tethered to reality despite the fantastical tale.

"Tiamat, the originator of all, held the tablets of destiny that gave her control over all things. But Ashur, feeling betrayed by her actions, took the tablets and wore them around his neck as a symbol of his newfound power and authority. With these tablets, he could dictate fate itself, shaping the world according to his will."

Her thoughts were like a feather lightly brushing against her mind, questioning the reality of the story being told. Ashur? Could he be so powerful that he overthrew the mother of creation?

As the sand passed beneath them, the scorpion man went on. "To protect his claim on destiny, Ashur, with the help of Daimon, built Atlantis — and it's heart the Temple of Destiny. Hidden beneath the undulating waves, where no one could reach or discover it, they lay in wait. With eyes as wise as time itself, he watched over the ebb and flow of centuries, creating the lineage of the Mer, ensuring they remained pure and protected from the outside world. They were a secretive and elusive race, hidden away from all others, their existence shrouded in mystery and magic. The underwater kingdom thrived in peace and isolation, untouched by the chaos and turmoil of the surface world above."

Zadie was struck with a wave of astonishment. Created? As her mind raced, she couldn't help but think back to the mysterious creatures she had seen in Atlantis, the ones that resembled both humans and creatures. Was she one of them—a hybrid, brought into existence from the depths of the ocean? A mere experiment, deemed worthy enough to have a chance at life? Could it truly be that it was the water-dragons, Sons of Tiamat, who had played a hand in the creation of the Merfolk. Could they really be her creators?

The scorpion man went on, not noticing her shock. "But when Tiamat decided to create eleven monstrous beasts to conquer and enslave humanity, Ashur could no longer ignore what was going on above the waves. He knew he had to act. Joining forces with Daimon, the last remaining water-dragon, they used their combined strength to create the Hall of Time. In this mystical realm beyond time and space, they captured Tiamat and all that served her, trapping them for eternity in this forgotten realm."

Zadie squeezed her eyes shut as a gust of wind kicked up a spray of sand, stinging her cheeks and getting into her hair. She gritted her teeth against the irritation and raised one hand to protect her face.

"Enough," interjected the storm demon, his voice like

the distant rumble of thunder. "Such knowledge is not for her ears."

Zadie turned her head toward the dark cloud of the storm demon, sensing the tension in the air that crackled with his disapproval. She held his gaze, or what she perceived to be his gaze, within the swirling vortex of his form. His command hung between them, a decree that brooked no argument.

As they edged along the vanished riverbank, life revealed itself in fleeting glimpses—a scuttle of iridescent beetles beneath a stone, a flash of a lizard's tail disappearing into a crevice.

It was then that Zadie's gaze caught sight of something extraordinary. On the horizon loomed an architectural marvel—a towering edifice spiraling toward the heavens. Its structure was reminiscent of a helix, windows wrapped around its circumference in an elegant dance of shadow and light. So massive was the tower that its pinnacle was lost to the azure expanse above.

"Is that . . . ?" Zadie trailed off, her eyes wide with wonder.

"The tower of the recorder of destinies," confirmed the scorpion man, following her gaze. "We are close now."

The sight of the colossal tower imbued Zadie with a sense of both awe and foreboding. It stood as a beacon amidst the desolation, an anchor in the shifting sands of their fractured timeline. As they approached, the very air seemed charged with importance, every grain of sand a silent witness to the countless fates entwined within the walls of that enigmatic citadel.

Even as her stomach lurched, Zadie knew there was no turning back now.

As the trio approached the formidable entrance of the tower, two figures emerged from the searing heat—a pair of colossal, winged bulls, their human faces etched with curiosity. The guardians of the threshold gazed upon them with eyes that had witnessed centuries pass by.

"State your purpose," rumbled one of the sentinels.

The scorpion man stepped forward, his tail arched defensively. "We seek an audience with the recorder of destinies," he implored, his voice betraying the gravity of their quest. Yet the guardians remained unmoved by his request.

It was the storm demon who broke the impasse, stepping forth as his form coalesced from a swirling sand cloud into a more discernible shape. "We bring Zadie of the Culebra line," he intoned, his soft lyrical voice slicing through the tension like a blade. "Her fate may be entwined with ours, and it must be proclaimed by the recorder."

The winged guards exchanged a glance that seemed to span an eternity before nodding assent. The gates creaked open, revealing an oasis within that defied the desolation that reigned beyond its borders.

As they stepped inside, the parched and unforgiving desert landscape melted away into a lush oasis of vibrant greenery. Hanging gardens stretched out in every direction, overflowing with foliage that spilled onto stone and wood structures in a wild array of colors. A cascading waterfall tumbled through the center of the sanctuary, its misty spray creating shimmering rainbows in the air. The air was heavy with the earthy scent of damp soil, mingled with the sweet fragrance of ripening fruits. It was a paradise amidst the barren wasteland, a reminder of nature's resilience and beauty.

"Drink," commanded the storm demon, gesturing toward the waterfall. The scorpion man obeyed without hesitation, cupping the crystalline water in his clawed hands before lifting it to his lips. He proceeded to anoint his head, the droplets catching the light as they slid over his carapace.

"Now you, Mer," said the storm demon, nodding to Zadie.

With a sense of apprehension, Zadie approached the waterfall, her hand trembling slightly as she scooped the water. She drank deeply, the cool liquid rejuvenating her parched throat. Following the scorpion man's example, she let the water trickle over her brow, the droplets mingling with the sand that coated her skin. She started as a sense of familiarity sparked in her consciousness—the water recognized her.

Their ritual complete, they turned to face the daunting ascent. The staircase wound around the exterior of the tower, ascending into the heavens like a serpentine path to the divine. Step by step, they climbed, the lush greenery of the gardens receding below them.

Zadie's muscles burned with exertion, each step heavier than the last. Her breath came in short gasps, her lungs begging for reprieve. She could feel the pull of delirium tugging at the edges of her consciousness, the world around her taking on a dreamlike quality as they spiraled upward.

"Keep going," urged the scorpion man, his voice soft yet commanding, a strange encouragement from one she deemed an enemy. But there was no time for reflection, only the relentless pursuit of what awaited them at the zenith of this helical marvel—the mysterious entity known as the recorder of destinies, whose words could proclaim the mysteries of existence.

With each laborious step, Zadie's resolve was tempered by the weight of the unknown. What would the recorder see in her destiny? Could the threads of her life be rewoven, or was she bound to the inexorable will of fate?

The climb was both a literal and metaphorical ascension, a journey toward answers that lay cloaked in the mists of uncertainty. And though her body cried out for rest, Zadie pressed onward, driven by the unspoken promise that at the summit, revelations awaited and perhaps — salvation.

Stumbling at the foot of two gigantic doors, Zadie's trembling hands traced the ancient glyphs carved into the jade monoliths, their cool touch a drastic contrast to the heat that still clung to her skin. She squinted at the indecipherable script, each line and curve as enigmatic as the depths of the ocean. "It looks like Ashur's necklace," she murmured, more to herself than her unlikely companions.

"Indeed," came the scorpion man's voice, a soft hiss. His clawed finger pointed to a jagged void near the base of the left door, where a shard of jade was conspicuously absent. "Ashur, the traitor, took it. A fragment of the Tablets of Destiny now adorns his neck, binding all worlds together."

Zadie pressed her palms against the cold stone, closing her eyes as a silent plea took form within her mind: Ashur, if you can hear me. I'm still alive. I'm still here. If you can hear me, tell my sisters I love them. The words were unspoken but fervent, a desperate incantation seeking the merest thread of connection from this prison to freedom.

As she withdrew her hands, the air around them grew dense.

"Are you prepared?" asked the scorpion man, his tone laced with an odd gentleness that belied his fearsome form.

"Is one ever truly prepared to face their fate?" Zadie replied, her voice steadier than she felt. Her gaze lingered on the intricate jade, pondering the paths her life had taken, the currents that had swept her into this alien realm.

With a solemn nod from the scorpion man, the moment arrived. The great jade doors began to part, a sliver of light infiltrating the dimness of the antechamber. Zadie braced herself, not for the end but for the revelation of what lay beyond.

Dear Reader,

I appreciate you taking the time to read this book. If you enjoyed it, would you kindly consider leaving me a review on your preferred retailer's website? Your feedback means a lot to me and helps more readers discover my work. Thank you for supporting me as an author!

Zadie's journey will continue in
Unusually Frazzled, Book One: Sons of Tiamat

Follow Nadine, Babs and Cricket in
Unfairly Pursued, Book Four: Culebra Chronicles

You can learn more about my books and subscribe to my newsletter at: www.chrissychicory.com

Follow me around the web

ACKNOWLEDGMENTS

A great team is essential to completing anything.

I would like to extend my sincere gratitude to the following individuals:

Cover design: Caroline Marques

Editing and Book Design/Typesetting: Enchanted Ink Publishing

Final editing: Rebeca Sams Willis

BOOKS BY CHRISSY CHICORY

Culebra Chronicles

Unabashedly Chosen, book 1
Seriously Challenged, book 2
Increasingly Complicated, book 3

CHRISSY CHICORY

hailing from of the sun-kissed shores of Daytona, has enraptured readers with her captivating Culebra Chronicles series. Inspired by a lifelong love for magic, comfort, and adventure, Chrissy mesmerizes readers with her fantastical stories that transport them to otherworldly realms and daring exploits. When she's not writing, she can be found exploring mysterious beach towns with her trusty Cavalier King Charles spaniel or engaging in lively conversations with fellow authors over lunch.

WWW.CHRISSYCHICORY.COM

www.ingramcontent.com/pod-product-compliance
Lightning Source LLC
Chambersburg PA
CBHW030820020726
47499CB00006B/2002